Mangtu Baba's House and Other Stories

Deepshikha Mehta

Copyright © 2024 by Deepshikha Mehta

All rights reserved.

This book or any portion thereof may not be reproduced or used in any manner whatsoever without the express written permission of the respective writer of the respective content except for the use of brief quotations in a book review.

The writer of the respective work holds sole responsibility for the originality of the content and The Write Order is not responsible in any way whatsoever.

Printed in India

ISBN: 978-93-5776-990-7

First Printing, 2024

The Write Order
A division of Nasadiya Technologies Private Ltd.
Koramangala, Bengaluru
Karnataka-560029

THE WRITE ORDER PUBLICATIONS.

www.thewriteorder.com

Typeset by MAP Systems, Bengaluru

Book Cover & Illustrations by Dalveer Singh

Publishing Consultant - Priyanka Lal

Contents

Disclaimer vii
Acknowledgments ix
Preface xi

Swimming with the Buffaloes 1
Mangtu Baba's House 9
Nandi and a Tonga Ride 21
Papa and Sheru 29
Bheenda's Little Secret 39
Krishan Chacha 47
For the Love of Mata! 59
Circuit House 67
An Unlikely Maverick 87
The Baoli 97

Afterword 109
Glossary 111

Disclaimer

This is a semi-fictional work containing some events, locales, and conversations from my memory. I may have changed the names of individuals, places, identifying characteristics and details. Any resemblance to actual persons, living or dead, or actual events is purely coincidental.

Acknowledgments

I would like to thank those who helped me in putting this book together. My mom, Sukarma Mehta for patiently clarifying facts and narrating tales to me as a storyteller in her own right. Dalveer for bringing these stories to life by capturing them in sketches and finally Tennessee Jones, my book editor for his valuable attention to detail.

Preface

With Love from Pitpita…

While helping my mother clear out the storeroom, I chanced upon a treasure — my father's journals from his childhood and adolescent years. I delved into them, creating a fictional world where fading memories merged with vivid dreams. Writing these stories helped me heal the wounds of losing my father. The ache of loss is constant but not without inspiration. I found peace in that.

Imagining your parents as kids is hardly desirable, some would say. I see the alarm on my son's face every time I begin a conversation with the words, "When I was your age…" His expression says it all — a bewilderment that transmits a message most parents rarely perceive: "Move on with it. You are a parent now. Please don't expect me to imagine you winning a race or performing on stage or dancing at a discotheque!"

I must have reacted to my father's stories in a similar fashion when he shared them with us. But I feasted on the precious notes, childlike pondering and honestly jotted incidents in the journals of Ramesh, the child who grew up to be my dad, when I found them as an adult.

I wanted to know what made him tick when he was growing up. Was he spunky or shy, adventurous or conservative, reserved or bubbly? The journals introduced me to my father as a curious kid who sought diverse experiences. They helped me connect the dots between papa's formative years and his parenting style. I understood better why my father had been relentless in introducing us to the world in all its vibrant forms. He exposed us to sports as diverse as sailing and hiking, and showed us Charlie Chaplin movies, as well as documentaries on lives of the greats as varied as Mahatma Gandhi and Abba! We read Charles Dickens, bilingual Russian magazines, and devoured works by Munshi Premchand, all thanks to him. He wanted us to taste all of life, past and present.

That he empathized with animals in their inability to communicate with humans was priceless, even if it came across as soppy, bordering on funny. During holidays he often disappeared into a poetic trance induced by hills and nature. For him, empathy and humility were a prerequisite for living, not an option. These were qualities I felt hard-pressed to emulate as a parent.

Distance that unintentionally grows between parents and children owing to attendant preoccupations of youth and aging is regrettable but universal. As I held the journals in my hands I saw in them an opportunity to bridge that distance. As a mother now, I connected with the journal entries differently than I would have in my youth. Being a parent brought me closer to my father at a time when he was no more.

Our relationship, like most parent-child relationships, had been far from perfect. Over the years, disagreements between us accumulated, solidified, melted, and reappeared like seasonal glaciers.

While I believe perfection is an illusion, even for the perfectionist who lives in it, Papa had an impeccable sense of the 'right' thing to do that made him different from us. He was quick to understand situations, emotions, and subtleties of feelings, and he expected the same of us. He had the uncanny ability of trusting and nagging us at the same time. In his journals I observed that he had absorbed emotional nuances early in life.

Curiosity can set a child apart from the giggling, scheming, screaming bunch that kids often become. You might find a curious child affected by the death of a bird, gazing at an unusual facial expression, or thinking deeply about oversights by adults. The environment is like a great novel for the curious child who loses herself in the story of life as it unfolds around her.

Papa was born in the tiny village of Kamahi Devi to an upper-class brahmin family that was respected for its contribution to the village economy. He was in awe of my grandfather, Babaji, who was the village headmaster. Middle-born with an elder brother and a kid sister, Papa got away with many childhood pranks. He was also his mother's (Mata's) favorite. Papa was the pampered one, as most responsibilities were shouldered by his elder brother. And he wasn't encumbered as his sister was by the social niceties that come with being a girl in those times. He was aware of this privilege but dared not misuse it for Babaji was a disciplinarian.

This collection of stories where Papa comes alive as Ramesh, the precocious child, contains elements of fiction. But the stories are rooted in reality based on lucent memories spanning the twenty-six years I spent with Papa.

Here, truth and story blend to create a fun-filled, introspective, and cathartic world. Each story is an effort to preserve memories on the brink of fading.

The desire to frame a moment or capture an event in slow motion are significant challenges for any chronicler. These fleeting moments are even more precious to me as my father's daughter.

All it takes for me to enter the recreated world of Ramesh is a slight push past the edge of the present and it's all there — the jumbo stones embedded in the path all the way from the bus stop to my grandparent's village house, shining with an earthy gloss from years of being grazed by leather shoes. The scraggly bushes lining the tiny farms, the towering lush trees, the echoes of pattering feet running on the sloped parapet that lined the outer wall of the house. Planning an afternoon caper in the shade of a mango tree in the backyard next to the barn, and basking in the elders' indulgences.

And there stands Ramesh utterly at peace with the insouciance that childhood comes with, living his own sunshine days.

Swimming with the Buffaloes

In those days swimming pools were few and far between, found only in the swankiest corners of cities. Most rural folk, in the early 1950s, had to make do with the village pond, which was called Toba in that part of the country.

Usually, village kids were not the only ones found frolicking around in the questionable waters of the Toba. Herds of buffaloes were active contenders for space as well. Animals and children swimming together were a fun sight, but not a healthy one. But this was a risk both parents and children took because options were limited.

Tobas fascinated me as a child. Similar reservoirs, also called Talaab in other regions, were a permanent feature in every village. I associated these with wildlife because I was used to swimming in the crystal clear and chlorinated waters of the Lake Club pool in Chandigarh. The thought of entering an opaque algae water body was unthinkable for me.

But I remember stepping into puddles on the road with guiltless abandon as a child, spraying my siblings with rainwater, inviting them to a puddle war. Like most adults, now I go around the puddles, tutting at kids who jump into them. This is an appalling side effect of 'growing up.' Hopping into water puddles is in a child's DNA!

Ramesh was about eight when he made for the village Toba without informing Mata, accompanied by his friends, Nikku and Cheela. It was the month of May, when the coolest corners of the mud-brick walls of the house failed to cool the torrid heat of mid-afternoon.

One of the features of village life is the fading away of human presence towards noon as nature's sounds emerge and human life sinks into siesta. On a sizzling summer day, you can hear the invading gusts of the Loo (dusty, hot, dry summer wind), the rustling of protesting leaves, and urgent fluffing of birds trying to cool themselves. As a teenager, I found this an ideal time to reflect on my piffling teenage worries. For adults, the afternoon is ideal for dozing. For children, it is a window to do as one wishes.

On one such afternoon, with the household doused in sleep, Ramesh stole out of the house in his shorts and chappal towards Nikku's house. Nikku was small for his ten years, and given Ramesh's red shining face and stocky built, Nikku quickly fell into the role of the follower. Being petite also had its advantages. Nikku, the brains behind their tiny gang's plans and pranks, easily slipped out from mind and sight of grown-ups. Ramesh, the one to okay or reject the ideas, held sway over his friends but bore the brunt of the adults' anger if they were caught.

Ramesh had instructed Nikku to 'borrow' certain things from home for the afternoon. Getting these objects for his best friend was a cinch for Nikku. It had been Ramesh's idea to go swimming in the Toba without the adults. "I am tall enough now to hold my face above the water with just a small push up from the Toba's floor," Ramesh had reasoned, arching up his body to test his claim. This would also work for Cheela, the third member of their group, but not for Nikku. But being a part of an escapade was all that mattered to Nikku.

"Did you get them?" Ramesh asked Nikku when he saw him carrying two thin and wiry wooden sticks. The sticks, meant to take on any over-friendly buffaloes in the Toba, had to be handpicked. The quality test called for swiping the stick diagonally to hear a cracking 'whoosh' slash the air. The sound itself was enough to warn the animals. They rarely had to use them unless an animal trespassed into Mata's garden. She was unforgiving in this matter.

Nikku handed a sieve to Ramesh to be used to catch rare, dead insects which would be stuck in a book to be safely preserved in Mangtu baba's backyard shed. A short walk brought them to Cheela, the third conspirator, waiting in the shade next to his house. Cheela had somehow gotten an old bicycle tire tube, which was patched but inflated. Ramesh could now prove his claim that he could stand in the deepest part of the Toba.

The Toba at three in the afternoon would be bereft of any human presence. About a twenty minute run from home, the quiet of the standing water body has its own still presence. Its waters looked mysterious, bordering on ominous. As they neared it, before Nikku and Cheela could back out, Ramesh rushed toward the water. He threw his towel on the ground nearby, and waded into the Toba waters in his shorts, holding the tube for support, his senses alert.

Nudging one's way past adult rules comes with its own charm and thrill. There's a level of risk assessment children are savvy to which adults often fail to appreciate, and for good reason. But for children, the fun of proving oneself correct is as good as winning a trophy.

Ramesh had been to the Toba many times with his elder brothers. In their comforting presence, he had learned to stay afloat. He had been warned of the presence of sharp-horned cattle many times, but his brothers protected the younger kids. After playing in the Toba, the kids would be herded to the nearest source of fresh water on the cobbled path. Mugs of water scooped from buckets would cascade down their hair and faces followed by a good rub with gooey brown homemade soap leaving the kids clean and sleepy. But the older brothers bossed them around, and Ramesh found this unfair.

He had been waiting for a chance to soak in the Toba without monitoring and threats from his brothers, and that day had finally arrived. Hot water of the Toba turned warm and then cool as he moved into its depths. The water level rose, reached his neck, and just as his toes left contact with the Toba's bottom, Ramesh turned onto his back. He held the tire tube around his torso like a circus acrobat's ring. He had mentally marked the center of the pond and kicked towards it.

Unknown to him, a huge buffalo with black curved horns was making its way from opposite side of the Toba to the coveted spot. Nikku and Cheela had paused to check the rim of the pond for wildlife, but Ramesh had been too busy feeling more important than his brothers to check for animals.

Upon surveying Ramesh's movement in the water, the buffalo paused.

"Look out, that's a nasty one," Cheela shouted, plonking himself on a mud hill under the Peepal tree next to the pond. Ramesh ignored Cheela's muffled voice.

He gave in to the granular water of the Toba flowing against his skin, the occasional weed brushing against his legs, the pebbles and stones poking his toes. He had wanted to swim in silence. Perhaps bringing friends along had not been a good idea.

This was the moment when Nikku took upon himself to wield the stringy sticks to scare away the buffalo. Nikku enjoyed terrorizing animals. The high point of the previous year's summer holidays had been a futile attempt at milking the mochi's goats. He could not resist the temptation of taking on the buffalo. Also, Ramesh would owe him big time. An inspired Nikku began a strange hopping dance, waving the sticks at the buffalo.

Meanwhile, the buffalo, after a lengthy survey, realized the kids were up to no good and lurched towards the centre of the Toba, straight towards Ramesh's head.

When he saw Cheela waving frantically from the bitty hill under the tree, Ramesh first thought it was a warning about one of his brothers or family elders approaching. He turned his head around on a whim to find bewildered eyes and pointed horns a few feet away from him. Ramesh felt his legs go as heavy as lead. Cheela and Nikku now stood unmoving, watching, their mouths agape.

This was when Ramesh heard a voice say, "Ramesh, get away, fast." Within seconds, he felt strong hands pull him to the side as the angry animal swam past, creating a muddy churn of water in its wake. Ramesh looked up to see a furious chacha, Babaji's youngest brother, as he pulled Ramesh towards the shore. Seeing that Ramesh was safe, Nikku made a clean escape through the nearby buddh, a forked gate used by people and goats to jump into a field. But Cheela, whose reflexes were a tad slower, felt his ear being twisted sharply. Ramesh received the same treatment, which caused both boys to yowl.

"What were you thinking?" chacha spat.

"We won't do it again," Cheela yelled.

"It was Nikku's idea," Ramesh said.

But chacha held on to their ears and marched them up to Babaji.

"Nikku will pay for this," Ramesh thought bitterly as he and Cheela took positions as murgas in the corner of Babaji's room.

But Nikku's cunning little brain knew perfectly well that his friends could not do without him. He had a plan to regain their loyalties, which involved inducing sympathy and offering an irresistible sweet treat.

The next time Nikku met Ramesh and Cheela, he sported a fake bandage on his leg. The dressing was fashioned from his mother's ripped up dupatta, which would inspire her fury when she later discovered what he'd done. But that bridge could be crossed later. Walking with a pretend limp, he offered them a conciliatory box of pedas he had swiped from the kitchen. His mission was a fait accompli. As they feasted on the pedas, Nikku explained how he had gotten hurt while jumping over the budh. His eyes danced with the audacity of the plan for their next adventure.

For Ramesh and Cheela, this combination was hard to resist. What neither of them knew was that their reconciliation was mostly due to the mercifully short-lived nature of childhood memory.

Mangtu Baba's House

With four brothers—Babaji and his three siblings—living together, the central courtyard of their house was perpetually abuzz with activity. It was a spread-out house, constructed from a mixture of mud, clay, concrete, and wood, with baked terracotta tiles for a roof. The structure of the house was average for those times, but the layout was lavish. The various aunts might be chatting while shelling peas, cleaning spinach, cutting vegetables, or rolling out cotton battis used in prayers. Or the courtyard might be filled by Ramesh's cousin sisters skipping rope, braiding each other's hair, playing hopscotch, or a toss-and-catch game of marbles.

The area was primarily a haunt for women and children unless an elderly male member of the house strolled in. There would be a flurry of activity where the girls would straighten up their act, and the aunts would pull down veils or ghoonghats over their heads, covering half of their faces. The whole concept of ghoonghat was archaic, and I found the veiled faces mystical. Chins of various shapes and sizes escaped the fringes of the ghoonghats, catching anyone straying into the courtyard off guard by the weird sense of authority that the ghoonghat clad women exerted.

Every house was referred to by a defining characteristic. Generally, it comprised the traits of the land where a house was built. If the ground sloped up to form a hill—as was the case where Cheela lived—it was called upparley ghar or "the upper house."

Sometimes, the house was named after the person living there. Formerly known by his grandfather's name as Shah Baba's house, Ramesh's home had recently been dubbed 'masterji's house.' No one registered when exactly the change had happened after Shah Baba passed away. You would be amicably guided to masterji's house by a willing passerby or inhabitant with a wave and a smile. Ensconced between the upper rise of the hill and the village of Garrey in the adjoining valley, Nikku's house was aptly named nicheley ghar, or "the lower house." It sat at the foot of the hillock.

On one of my visits to the village when I inquired about some people we had met in Kamahi marketplace one day I was told in a hushed tone that mochis lived in a particular part of the village. It was a disturbing thought for a child. Adults mingled in the market, waving salutations, exchanging news on wellbeing, and then they returned to their high castles defined by caste.

The liberal, equality-seeking spirit in me rebelled, but it was a system that seemed to work for the villagers. Over the years as I grew older I sensed a harmonious understanding that allowed communities a space to live, enjoy, or mourn. There was no animosity. Though I remain skeptical to date for one grave casualty of the caste-based housing—an unspoken agreement that children should form their separate playgroups. Watching children submit to such rules doesn't make for a pretty sight. However, they are simply following the codes of conduct that their elders had never questioned.

But what happens when a child chances upon a spirit that echoes his or her own?

Bheenda was one such spirit who got along well with Ramesh and the rest of the group, though he came from the mochi caste. Bheenda was usually part of the group in the absence of elders. Nothing was ever said about it. Bheenda was nicknamed for his likeness to a 'ladyfinger'—he had a sallow expression, a mop of hair prone to standing out like grass, and a narrow tapering body. He did a disappearing act the moment grown-ups approached.

I would never know if this affected Ramesh. What I do know is that as a father, he was rarely ever condescending or harsh towards people based on their vocation. The gardener, sweeper, or any other worker rarely left our home without being served a cup of tea by a grumbling mom who saw no reason for uncalled hospitality at the expense of her time and effort.

One day, Ramesh, Nikku, Cheela, and Bheenda felt overly adventurous. Committing acts bordering on taboo, albeit based on child-like risk assessment, is something that is lost when one grows up. It is also the one feature common to all gleeful gangs of children, whether geeky or bratty.

Overlooking the entrance steps into masterji's house was an arched gateway made of thorny branches. This was the threshold into Mangtu baba's house. I suspect that these thick and twisted boughs had initially been wild rose bushes strung to form an arch that had eventually hardened into an ebony spiky guardian for the lonely old man's fortress. I never saw any flowers on them. As a child, when I visited my grandparents, my first impression of the house was 'ready to fall and probably haunted.' Once, I stared at it long enough to get spooked by it. The two-story mud house with wooden fittings and its main door and windows hanging on their hinges seemed to sneer at me like an eccentric witch.

The house was neater when Ramesh was young. But the garden around the house remained the same. Even then it was unkempt, bramble and weeds rampant, an occasional out of place wildflower tussock dressing up the landscape.

A crudely hammered wooden bench was like a safe island in this wild undergrowth. The house possessed a quiet and ominous presence, but rather than scare away Ramesh and his three buddies, it kindled mystery in them. Especially the garden, which appealed as a perfect hideaway to mischievous kids desperately in need for a break from the grown-up world. The unruly grass and weeds in the yard seemed to call out to the kids, inspiring them to let go of their inhibitions, offering themselves as models for the rebel within each child.

The house and the garden were components of an ideal childhood adventure-fantasy, an Indian village's answer to the coveted treehouses of the West. Needless to say, the concept of 'space for children' was a lost cause in the adult world at that time. Kids had to secure that place by themselves. Unknown to Mangtu baba, his garden had a tiny hidden gateway in the form of a large hole in the bramble hedge. Stuffed with dry sticks when not in use, the hollow was invisible to prying eyes, and sufficiently thorny to repel an inquisitive goat.

Most adults prefer children play by themselves. But if you look closely, you find that every child has a hiding place that is messy and shunned by adults, where the child feels most secure for pretend-play with toys and imaginary friends or dealing with situations that have irked them or gone unexplained. Modern-day living has reduced this earnest, joyful solitary intimacy to cramped quarters under a table or behind a cabinet. But this space is important for kids, even if underrated and misunderstood by adults.

One day, it came to pass that Mangtu baba was set to make a trip to the central marketplace of Kamahi about 10 km from the village. The cobblestoned winding path and summer heat added the equivalent of another 5 km to the journey. For most families, such trips were a full-day affair. Mangtu baba was a reclusive, introverted soul you could hardly call the hail-fellow-well-met type. Unknown to Ramesh, Mangtu baba had a history that cushioned the effects of his behavior and lifestyle on those around him.

This dates back to early 1900s when Mangtu baba's father was married. As the only son, Mangtu baba's father, Bali Chand, had seven sisters to support. To the chagrin of his parents, Bali Chand failed to produce an heir. Perpetual goading and coaxing to marry a second time forced Bali Chand to adopt a child, the son of his wife's cousin. The child was readily named Mangtu—derived from the Hindi word mangna or 'to ask.'

But this was not enough for Bali's mother, who demanded a natural heir. Mangtu's father married again. As the family celebrated, his first wife and Mangtu were relegated to the cold and non-festive corners of the house. Mangtu was also reduced to the role of a helping hand in the house at a very young age. Soon, the second wife bore a son, but the flurry of joy reversed to a sorrow just as intense. The second wife and the baby succumbed to tuberculosis. Mangtu's father went into depression and never recovered. Mangtu took the physical abuse and work for granted, oblivious of the crimes for which he was being punished. Scorned as a child by a resentful dadi (grandma), Mangtu lost track of the moments when those responsible for his pitiable existence passed away one by one. When he became the master of the house at the age of 35, he kept working as a slave in his own home.

Mangtu failed to register the vacuum created by the deaths of his father, mother, and dadi. He was too busy loathing himself and the world around him, which he perceived to be a mirror reflection of his own unloving family. Rumors regarding the disappeared bodies of Mangtu's grandmother and father spread like fire, which then faded into wisps of whispers before turning into tepid folklore. Years later when Ramesh inquired if there was any truth to hearsay, Babaji rubbished all gossip connected with Mangtu baba.

Nobody thought about getting Mangtu married. None could bear to sentence their daughters to a wretched life in that unpropitious house. This was how Mangtu baba, at the age of 50, came to be a grumpy old bachelor, left to his fate by the world. His only socializing came from the monthly trip to Kamahi, which he made for household supplies—food, wood, other building material for house repairs, and seeds for the kitchen garden, the only patch of land both inside and outside the house that had any semblance of nurturing.

Ramesh and his three amigos could easily guess the day and date of Mangtu baba's junket. This time it would be Tuesday. The group had elaborate plans to go through Mangtu baba's barn. The barn was tucked away in the farthest corner of the backyard and

connected with the front garden from one side of the house. The other side wall of the house marked a boundary for the property. The barn housed no animals.

It was a ramshackle creaking structure on the verge of collapse but still stood because of the two thick main logs supporting it. Covered on three sides, the barn was dark, eerie, and as uninviting as possible. But rather than frighten them, it lured them in like a spell-casting harpy. That the barn was off limits for the kids tempted them to explore it. They had already been caught peeking in once and had tasted Mangtu baba's wrath.

In its own twisted way, the barn resembled Mangtu baba. His eyes were always screwed up, the livid expression on his face amplified by an abundance of wrinkles, and his lengthy lips stretched towards both ears in a grimace that showed his bitter personality. In fact, a bit of the fear Mangtu baba inspired rubbed off on all the material things around him.

When Tuesday came, Nikku hid behind a bush close to the house to see Mangtu baba off. Mangtu baba held a wooden staff firmly in his hand to tackle any adventurous reptiles searching for breakfast and wore a Himachali cap on his head. Nikku emerged from hiding when he saw his bobbing head disappear over the cobbled pathway.

The sun was out and all set to follow its unhurried early winter itinerary. Nikku dashed to Ramesh's house next door just as Ramesh was finishing his morning paratha breakfast. On seeing Nikku, Ramesh quickly rolled two parathas with some pickle. He planted one roll in Nikku's hand, and together they marched to Cheela's house before Mata could fire a volley of questions. Dripping with homemade butter and spicy pickle, the savory parathas slowed their pace, not their plans.

The trio was met by Bheenda outside the backyard of Mangtu baba's house. With Mangtu baba out of the picture for a few hours, they needn't have snuck in through their regular mode of entry, but they feared being seen by adults.

They entered the garden, the four of them feeling thrilled as they cautiously made their way to the barn. Each expected to discover something fantastic that day. Nikku was sure they would meet the ghosts of Mangtu baba's father and dadi.

Though he refrained from sharing this with the others for fear of being mocked, Cheela expected to find a hoard of precious jewels or trinkets. Bheenda secretly wanted to find some books on history. But Ramesh had left his imagination blank. He wished to discover Mangtu baba through the items in his barn.

When they pulled the flimsy hay and bamboo door aside, huge yellow brass jars greeted them. Dull from years of disuse, the jars managed only a pale gleam in response to sunlight. Beckoned by these towering keepers of secret treasure the kids rattled the jars in excitement their imagination getting ahead of them their hopes unyielding even when the jars turning out to be empty.

Bheenda ventured into the darkest corner of the shack and came away with a trophy for his risk — a sword, slightly curved like a scimitar. The weapon had belonged to Mangtu's father, who had carried it with him on his trading trips to Kabul. Admiration welled up in the foursome, which took away any leftover shreds of inhibition.

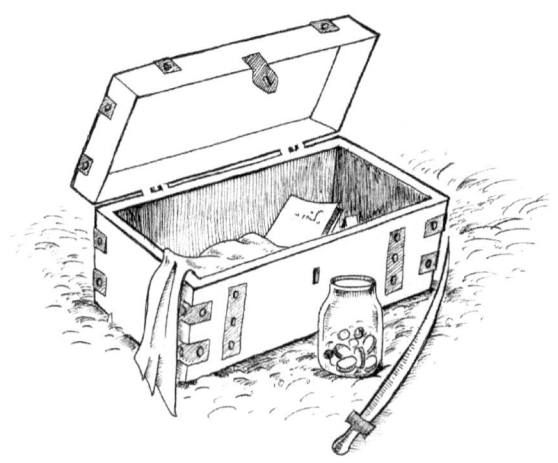

A sense of joy compelled them to keep exploring. They overturned stone pots, which spilled out a handful of old and heavy coins to the utter delight of kids. In an old trunk, they found some moth-eaten jackets and a silk dupatta. Bheenda lucked out when they extracted a hand-illustrated book on horses from the chest, written in the Urdu language.

An early morning escapade extended into the afternoon, every second strung like a bead to create a precious memory for them, especially for Ramesh who felt the joy of the day more than anyone else. Apart from having discovered the treasure of bric-a-brac trashed by adults, there was another reason this day was special for Ramesh.

Of the four, Ramesh feared Mangtu baba the most. Ramesh rarely ventured close to the entrance of his house after dark. He would avert his eyes if he and Mangtu baba ever chanced across each other. But this escapade had changed things. The scary barn turned out to be harmless. They had found no ghosts or dead bodies. Foraging through the remotest corner of Mangtu baba's house had taken the sting out of his grouchy looks and cranky demeanor. At the end of the day, Mangtu Baba was just a regular oddball. There was no evil side to him now.

The three friends and a reluctant Nikku decided that they would not take the rewards of their labor home, but would stash them in a corner. All coins went into one jar and the sword into another. The contents of the trunk were carefully placed back where they'd found them. Taking these would have amounted to stealing, and they could always come back and play with them once a month when Mangtu baba visited the Kamahi market.

Nikku suggested burying the treasure for a treasure hunt later, but Ramesh the son of a headmaster prevailed. He wanted nothing to disturb the mysterious fabric of this spot which held the promise of turning into a haunt for their gang.

That evening when Mangtu baba visited Babaji for an evening stint of hukkah, Ramesh skipped up to him and said, "Ram, Ram baba."

Taken aback by the child's friendliness, Mangtu baba smiled and what a smile it was. With half his teeth gone, his remaining teeth were like flowers in the wilderness of his ridged face, matched only by eyes that lit up within folds of skin around them.

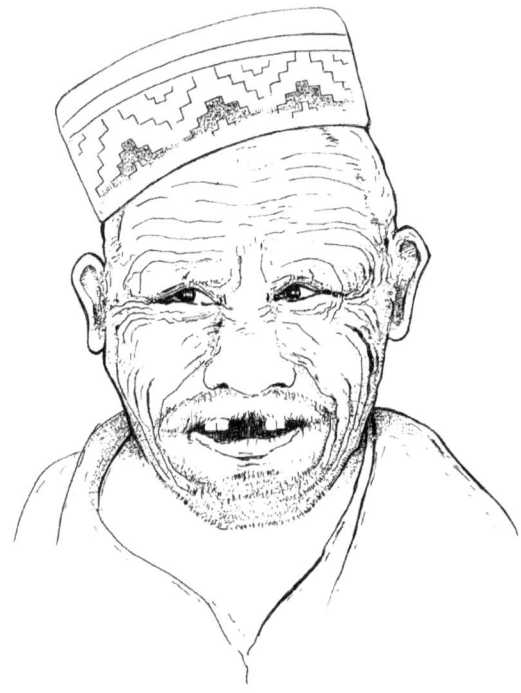

When we were kids, Papa discouraged us from visiting Mangtu baba's house and the garden that lay in shambles after Mangtu baba died. Papa believed that together nature and people can lighten misfortunes and ravages of time. But without life, there were no threads to join the material world around us, no bonds to forge.

I sensed in him a fear of facing these memories. Perhaps he wanted to shield us from the permanence of ruin, from pain.

It was much later that I discovered the bond between him, Mangtu baba, and Mangtu baba's garden. And along with pain, the memory brought joy.

Nandi and a Tonga Ride

"Will you go with bua or do you want to come with me to my office?" Babaji asked Ramesh. Now, the same question had been offered to him many times. Each time, an emphasis on a different word and accompanying facial expressions provided Ramesh with a clue to Babaji's preference in the matter. If Babaji stressed 'office' with an encouraging smile and raised eyebrows, it promised opportunities to interact with the office clerk, visit empty classrooms, play with chalk, run down to the barn to feed the animals, or have the thick rope-swing fitted on the old mango tree in the playground all to himself.

If the word 'office' was muttered plainly, without the inviting expressions, this meant the best bet for fun would be bua's place, where there were other boys his age. This time around, Babaji, intent on reading official papers in his hand, hardly looked up. Clearly, he didn't want Ramesh at the office.

"I want to go to bua's house," Ramesh said.

Babaji glanced at Mata. She muttered disapprovingly because this would mean an overnight stay at bua's house in Daulatpur, a village which was a three hour-long tonga ride from Kamahi. Bua ruffled Ramesh's hair fondly as he rushed to throw together a few essentials for his overnight stay. He quickly returned to stand beside his visiting bua so Mata couldn't suggest a change of plans.

A patchwork of trails marked the way to bua's village. Cobblestones all over Kamahi were difficult to cross unless one rode a horse. Thereon gravel and paved roads alternated. I remember how the entire family walked the guests to the periphery of Kamahi. By the end of the walk, pleasantries and one's breath had both ran out.

A tonga was waiting for them when they reached their goodbye spot. Tired from the walk, Ramesh hurried into the tonga. Krishan chacha, the household's man Friday, helped bua with her luggage. In those days, waving goodbye and long farewells were not the norm. The family had already turned to leave when the driver clucked at the horses to get them moving.

Tongas are a rare sight nowadays, but if they were still around, I wonder how kids would react to them. There's a sense of contentment in the gait and speed of the tonga, the heady tapping of the horses' hooves combining with the sights and sounds of stories exchanged on the way. There's also an ample opportunity for kids to frisk about the tonga, to bound off it to pluck pebbles. Catching up with the tonga to swing oneself overboard and aim shots at passing objects was Ramesh's favorite play.

Ramesh was ready for the breezy journey ahead. He would wait for the pebbled path, where he would take short skips off the tonga. Mostly, the tongas used by the general public were bare, drawn by a caparisoned horse to attract travelers. But this tonga was special, with luxe interior. Bua had married into one of the wealthiest families in the area, and the interior came with a soft-cushioned seat, pillows, pakhis, and a tiny window embellished with a pretty curtain. Bua was small framed, with kind eyes and a determined mouth. Dressed in a satin sharara and shirt, she shifted deeper under the canopy to make more room for Ramesh to lie down.

But Ramesh was thinking of adventure. He liked challenges, but what he valued more than winning was fun. He rarely picked large objects like tree trunks or boulders to target with his pebbles. Instead, he would choose a thin green branch jutting from the broad spread of a tree, a teenie-weenie mango bud, or an unsuspecting insect perched on a leaf or a stone. And if he missed, which was the case most of the times, he didn't take it to heart. His focus increased when the task got harder, which made the journey seem shorter.

Alas, the adventure was not to be, for tonga rides are also ideal for power naps. In the cool shade of the canopy, made breezier with bua's hand-held pakhi, snoozing was unavoidable. The best way to enjoy the luxury of a pakhi was when someone else took up the task of swinging it. Ramesh's fawning bua was only too happy to do this. The melodic clippetty-clop of the horse's hooves and the tinkling ornaments lulled him into a pleasant sleep, smoothing over the jarring bumps on the way. The next thing Ramesh knew, he was being gently shaken to be told that he had arrived at bua's house.

"Drats! I missed skipping off the tonga." Ramesh looked grouchily at bua. Unaware of her nephew's resentment, bua patted Ramesh appreciatively when he helped the tonga driver with the luggage.

Daulatpur is a village with commercial overtones, and if the village folk aspired for it to turn into a bustling town, this was well-justified. Just as ancient civilizations grew around rivers because of commerce, in present times, newer towns started as villages hugging an arterial road on both sides. From these, smaller towns bubbled up as a school, sometimes a college or a hospital were added to the public infrastructure.

Daulatpur had lucked out amongst other such villages. The shops lining the main road provided a buffer for the residential areas behind them.

Farther away from the principal road, the local school and college buildings marked the outer boundary of the town. Nowadays, a deluge of youngsters spills on to the market street in the evening—visiting temples, shopping for groceries, buying bangles, dropping by salons, or just gadding about for gossip.

The well-heeled populace of the village that could afford land right off the arterial road owned palatial houses with central courtyards. Bua's house, built on one such fine spot, boasted contemporary architecture. Concrete balustrades were the rage in those times, and bua's house brandished the bulkiest ones. Its three storeys built of cement, with light-blue and yellow facade, would inspire awe in any onlooker. But Ramesh ran straight inside without so much as a glance at it. He was cut short in his sprint by Nandi, bua's third born, who was a year younger than Ramesh.

Children rarely base their friendships on falsities like clothes, appearances, or salutations. There's an instant tuning of thoughts and movement towards a plan of action that makes them think, "He or she is all right."

Nandi beckoned Ramesh to follow him, and Ramesh unquestioningly did so. They dashed towards an unclaimed mango tree on an abandoned piece of land nearby.

The mango tree laden with comforting bunches of raw mangoes appeared to flaunt its independence, like an artist intent on adding a touch of paisley to the drab small-town garb.

Ramesh remembered traveling far from home in Kamahi to collect ripe mangoes from trees growing on the edges of farmland or unclaimed land. "The trees have been paid for by us," Babaji would explain. Perhaps the owner of this tree lived far from it too. Before Ramesh could ponder more, Nandi spoke, "Let's see who can take down the maximum number of mangoes." Nandi had picked up the first stone to aim at the mangoes.

Ramesh lost no time, the travel fatigue dissipated. They collected a pile of stones to aim at the bigger mangoes and within an hour had a heap of a dozen. Fearing reprimand, they stashed five mangoes in various pockets and carried the rest as an offering to appease the elders.

Nandi handed over the entire load to Ramesh who made straight for the kitchen and delivered them to bua. Her sisters-in-law gushed over Ramesh and promised to make mango chutney for him to take back home. Before dinner, bua pushed Ramesh towards Phuphaji—a regal man with sharp eyes laced with kindness. He wore tiny gold loops in his ears, which added history to his character. Ramesh said a quick namaste, and was about to escape when Phuphaji caught him by his arm and made Ramesh sit next to him on the rope mesh bed, which was called manji in village parlance. Ramesh noted that even the manjis in bua's house were fancy. The bedposts had colorful tassels, and the legs of the bed-frame were carved.

Ramesh shared with Phuphaji news about wellbeing of Babaji, his own age, grade and related tidings, and then endured another half hour of village polity and details of various land deals being discussed between Phuphaji and other elders. Before long, bua came to his rescue and announced it was time for the kids to have their dinner. In those days, respecting elders was a norm. It was not a value taught to children in bullet points or moral science classes. Children just never looked their parents in the eye. They did their parents' bidding and stayed out of the elders' way. If they did not, they would be judged, and that is not easy for any generation.

Ramesh hastened to the kitchen where bua's brood of six children patiently waited for the guest. In families with more than four children, an interesting sibling politics was at work at all times. Ramesh was their first cousin, but with cliques, close bonds, and fights amongst themselves, it was easy for him to be a fly on the wall. Ramesh wondered if anyone, except for bua, would notice if he disappeared. Similarly back home, Babaji and his brothers all living together had made it difficult for children to distinguish who was their real sibling and who wasn't.

Even though he was an outsider to this group, Ramesh liked this change because he got along well with Nandi. With four sons and two daughters, bua's kitchen resembled a school mess. They sat on the floor in two rows, cross-legged, on home-woven cotton runners. Nandi gestured to Ramesh to sit next to him. As Ramesh sat next to him, Nandi nudged a small mango, washed and peeled, towards Ramesh, and they both grinned. Stuti, the second youngest of the six whimpered, "I want mango too." A reluctant Nandi passed one mango to his little sister. Archana, the eldest, duly poured water for everyone.

Gender discrimination can be seen somewhat differently if one looks at the setting in bua's house closely. Phuphaji was the wealthiest man in the village, and most in love with his two daughters, Archana and Stuti. When he didn't encourage them to study, it was not due to lack of love, but because of sheer indulgence.

"What is the need for her to work so hard, poring over books and taking exams when she will one day get married into a rich household and live like a queen?" Phuphaji argued. Still, bua, who had felt the handicap of not having attended school, sent her daughters to school and then college, in the nearest town of Talwada, where her maternal aunt lived. Archana completed her Bachelor of Arts, followed by a Bachelor in Education after she got married. Stuti grew up to be a gold medalist in Sociology. Ramesh's own sister, Anandini, whom he had left crying behind, had similarly scraped together a degree. Ramesh woke up the next morning with an eager Nandi waiting to take him around the village before he had to go back home.

They set off with Bholu, the youngest sibling, following them around like a faithful puppy. If ever you've visited your relatives or extended family as a child you'll remember how different a child's idea of sightseeing is from that of grown-ups.

Childhood excursions include climbing walls, playing with cuddly kittens or a road mongrel's puppies, playing hide and seek in the crumbling ruins of abandoned houses, and raiding mango or guava trees. For Ramesh the day was so packed that he jotted down the details of the most enjoyable fatigue in his journal lest the memories faded away later.

Little did Ramesh know that the fragments of such capers would resurface and shape his attitude when his kids stepped warily towards trees. He would encourage us, to my mother's horror, to scale the tree trunks without help. He wanted to see the same flicker of joy on our faces that was buried in some corner of his heart. A flight of soul one experiences in early years, a brick in a child's palace of happy thoughts.

Papa and Sheru

Papa's attachment to dogs has all the elements of a Bollywood pot-boiler. Some of my fondest memories are of discussions with papa about dogs—a story that he had read somewhere or a tiny gesture that a guest pet in the house may have shown.

"He came and complained to me when I got home," Papa once said about a dog temporarily stationed at our house. "No one plays with him."

These stories amused us, for the guest dog was just an animal and Papa an animal lover. We were unable to understand his emotions beyond these categories. Not until I reached college did I discover that there was a story within the story.

The first time I saw Papa cry was when he was narrating a story about a man whose dog had strayed. The owner of the dog put up flyers and announced a reward for anyone who finds and returns his dog. When he received a call from the person who had found and adopted the dog mistaking him for a stray, the man felt overwhelmed. Excited to meet his best friend, the man reached the dog's new home only to find him engaged in play with the new owner. While hidden behind the gate, he whistled a tune, sure that his dog would remember, but the dog showed no sign of recognition and continued to play with its new owner. The heartbroken man expressed his wish to let the dog stay with his new master despite the new owner's insistence that the dog would settle down in a few days if brought back to its original home. The new owner could sense the man's pain.

I saw streams of tears run down Papa's cheeks as he told this story, standing at the threshold of the kitchen as Mom and I prepared the afternoon tea. That day I realized that the heart ruled over the mind for Papa. I could also sense that seeing his kids leave to lead their own independent lives would be tough for him.

In this light, it is important to share the story of Chota — a Great Dane inappropriately named Chota meaning 'tiny' in Hindi. Left with us by our family friends who were moving abroad for work, Chota was gigantic and ate more than the entire family put together. He also earned the reputation of literally being the 'bête noire' in our neighborhood. Whichever room the family lounged in, Chota also sprawled across the divan or the sofa. We soon realized the dog was ill-fitted to live with a vegetarian family in city accommodation. That Chota be put up for adoption was a difficult but unanimous decision. The only one wrecked by it was Papa, who claimed that Chota knew what was about to happen and therefore had not eaten for two days. Further discussions and negotiations resulted in Papa setting one condition—Chota would be handed over to someone who owned a farm on city outskirts. And yes, the new owner would undergo a grueling interview.

The completion of the project followed two rescue missions where Chota was traced to fake adopters. For one rescue mission, a police constable helped track down the fraudsters who had posed as farm owners. The other adopter had pretended to own a large house while he had wanted Chota only to intimidate the neighborhood surrounding his single-room quarters. All of this was guided by Papa and his 'gut instincts.'

Finally, a suitable adopter visited us. Having read the advertisement Papa had placed in the local newspaper, the man had come prepared with references from people known to Papa. He owned a large farm on the outskirts of the city, and Chota warmed up to him instantly. We were all rooting for this man who had handled dogs before. Personally, I was sure he was the right choice when he promised Papa to take excellent care of Chota. He even invited Papa to visit any time he wanted. We all knew that would never happen.

After Chota left that day, Papa refused to eat dinner. He wept as food lay before him, and the entire family looked on, nonplussed. That was how Papa acted when it came to goodbyes that had a sense of permanence to them. A stoic non-reaction in Papa met news of a death in family or friends. The coexistence of such extreme realism and childish sensitivity in one person intrigued me.

I later chanced upon the story of Sheru, papa's childhood pet, a fierce sheepdog bred by the Gaddis of Himachal. Narrated to me by my bua, Papa's teary-eyed sister, the anecdote filled in the blanks for me. It helped me connect with my own pet, the cynosure of my kids' eyes.

Gaddis are nomadic tribes of the mountainous state of Himachal Pradesh. They are well-known for domesticating an aggressive breed of Gaddi dogs. Loyal pets and efficient guards of livestock, Gaddi dogs are powerful enough to fight off a snow leopard.

On one of his work-related trips, Phuphaji brought Nandi and Ramesh to Palampur—a beautiful, verdant place with grass-carpeted, undulating hills pricked by hundreds of spear-like pine trees concealing multiple sparkling waterfalls.

It was here that, at the age of thirteen, Ramesh first met a group of Gaddis who had camped on a nearby mountainside. Bulky nose-rings and jutting headgear were part of the Gaddi women's attire, and sand-colored pattu overalls worn by the men struck Ramesh as adventurous. These elements reminded him of carefree, rough-weathered wanderings. Years later, while practicing law at district courts in Dharamshala, Ramesh would turn into a shutterbug, clicking away at the captivating everyday lives of Gaddi people.

While Phuphaji attended to business, he left Nandi and Ramesh under the careful supervision of Belaram, the chief surveyor in the employ of Phuphaji. Bored by Belaram's incessant chatter, which was punctuated by orders given to workers at the construction site, Ramesh and Nandi decided to explore the hills.

They dodged Belaram and ran over the hill to the opposite slope where they chanced upon a Gaddi camp. Warmly received by the campers, they were soon happily biting into homemade savories served with goat's milk. Perched on tiny stools made of wood and leather, Ramesh spotted a young herder running down the hill with a stout black dog in pursuit. When he reached the camp, the young man stopped short and slumped on the grass to trick the dog into leaping over and across his body. Having anticipated the act, the dog too halted, leapt and landed squarely on the young man's chest and took his wrist in its mouth.

Ramesh and Nandi watched while the young herder lolled on the grass gleefully, enjoying the playful nipping by the dog. The boy who went by the name of Dholki relished having won the race with his pet dog Rani. Ramesh got up and slowly approached the duo, fascinated by the scope of play that owning a pet provided and genuinely interested in knowing whether this involved getting your hand bitten off.

Dholki instantly noticed the affection for animals in the children's eyes, and took Ramesh and Nandi to meet Rani's four new pups—balls of fur with sparkling black stones for eyes. The puppies clamored to make friends with the children under Rani's trusting watch. When a puppy escaped his overbearing siblings to hide in Ramesh's palm, the magic of love at first sight happened. From that day onwards that puppy had Ramesh in his padded paw.

Ramesh named him Sheru after the resemblance of Gaddi dogs to majestic lions. Sheru had taken after his mother— all black with specks of white at the tips of the hair that covered his ears and back, with a large patch of white fur on his neck.

"Would masterji allow you?" Phuphaji had asked Ramesh while coldly putting down Nandi's request to keep a pet.

"He loves dogs," Ramesh replied. After all, Babaji had provided shelter to a stray on school premises. Still, butterflies hit his tummy hard as he held Sheru to his chest during the return trip. To his relief, Babaji smiled at the fresh addition to the family. Mata muttered something like, 'Who will make the rotis to feed a Gaddi dog?' The kids in the family simply screamed with delight.

For the first few months, Sheru was the darling of the family. He received pats from the elders, a morsel or two from Mata and chachis, and played games of tag with the kids. Ramesh rarely ever felt possessive like other kids his age might have. In fact, that Sheru was to be a member of the Mangtu Baba's garden gang was understood from the moment he set his paw into the house.

And all the while, Sheru hardly left Ramesh alone. A lick in the morning, and reassuring snores or grunts during the night told Ramesh that Sheru was near. At times, he even preferred Sheru over Nikku and Cheela, such as when he sneaked out with Sheru up to the lush hillside beyond the rocky and barren land called kapade. Uninhabited and mostly deserted, the hillside provided a perfect spot of soft ground to run around with abandon. Sometimes they would chance upon wild peacocks strutting around, at other times alert rabbits.

Mostly it was just silence and nature. Ramesh would race Sheru to a tree, and if he saw Sheru overtaking him, he would quickly turn back. Sheru would spin around joyfully with his ears pressed back, unaware that Ramesh had turned the tables against him, happy to be chasing his favorite playmate. Now and then, Ramesh would sit on a fallen tree branch to watch Sheru chase insects, sniff the air after butterflies, or scare away the birds. Deep down in his heart, he believed that Sheru could not want to eat these creatures—he was just incorrigibly playful.

It was Sheru who gave birth to an unadulterated feeling of love and understanding for creatures who can't speak for themselves in Ramesh. Though Sheru was 'just a dog' to other family members, Ramesh saw much more in him—a free spirit, a loyal friend, and a playful child.

The Gaddi breed characteristic in Sheru surfaced whenever there was a stranger around. Such occasions were few because a village in those times was one extensive family. For women, dropping in to exchange a juicy piece of news was a daily affair. Every so often members of the same family would call to update Mata and other women about gossip that covered Kamahi and nearby villages—a recent marriage, the gold that the bride wore, whether a certain bride had conceived, or perhaps she could not bear children and the tragedy of this! A common cold would have Mata's friends dropping in with their own variations of home remedies. Women had their own ways of social networking those days.

For men, the timing of the meetings mattered. By the evening, manjis would be laid out in a straight line, their occupants stretched out, with heads resting on rolled-up turbans serving as pillows, bodies unmindful of the harsh rope used to weave the manjis digging into their dry and weatherworn skins. On my visits to the village, the rugged and coarse feel of the manjis would have a city resident like me instantly wishing for a soft foam mattress and air-conditioning.

Masterji's house, like many others in those days, was divided into four wings. At the entrance itself, you would find yourself in a large rectangular room called dyodhi. Manjis belonging to Babaji and his brothers lined the walls. Above each bed, a small nook in the wall proved handy to keep one's book or a glass of water. Adjoining the dyodhi was the baithak, or drawing-room. A place of pride and stature then, as in modern times, the baithak was the most underutilized space in the house, meant only for entertaining guests who came for official reasons such as land deals and marriage proposals. It was in the dyodhi that the day's happenings would be discussed, and visitors entertained. As night fell, cotton-wool mattresses and pillows would be set on these manjis.

Crossing over to the right from the dyodhi, through a pleasant courtyard which was neither too big nor too small, one would find the women's quarters. Each mother had a separate set of two rooms for herself and the kids. Across from the dyodhi was a two-storied mud house that stored about 10-15 pots—earthen and brass—filled with drinking water ferried from a baoli, about 2 km away from home. Baolis were deep-set wells with steps, sometimes over a hundred, leading from surface level to water.

The water-storage unit in the building contained many shelves made of clay. Craters carved into these shelves for water pots were lined with wet jute cloth to help cool the water. There was a complete absence of life in this building, which rendered it creepy. I remember visiting the spot late in the evening once, only to get spooked by the silence, and brass pots large enough to hide a monster or a ghost. Hill folk believed in such tales.

Adjoining this building was the kitchen, which had an attached seating space outside with a roof, like an extensive porch without furniture. Every morning, having swept the porch with a handy little broom fashioned out of hay, one would shake open runner rugs for family members to sit on for their meals.

To the left of the dyodhi and the courtyard was a tiny farm, too big to be called a kitchen garden, used to grow vegetables for home use. Today, a newly constructed wing stands in that space. 'Made in cement,' Mata proudly informed our neighbors and relatives while visiting us in the city.

In those days a rugged path cut through this farm and was mainly used by women who preferred to avoid the primary entrance, where they were bound to bump into a male family member. One rarely saw a stranger enter the house through this path. And Sheru had observed this.

Sheru's behavior can thus be attributed to an inborn instinct that neither he nor the person who got bitten could have controlled. Mata's niece was visiting for a few days. Her husband had been to the house a few times, but Sheru had been a little pup during those visits. He was now three with sharp reflexes due to his heredity and the physical exercise he got with Ramesh and his cronies.

When the son-in-law of the house took the shortcut into the house in the dying light of the day, oil lamps had already been lit, which cast long shadows. Sheru leapt at him with the precision of a policeman nabbing a thief.

The man's yowls fell on horrified ears. The next day Sheru was given a rude send-off by a furious Babaji who waved away all pleas by the kids on Sheru's behalf. Babaji's parting words were, "The animal is a menace!" Fortunately, Ramesh was not around to hear this unfair statement. He had been sent to Talwada for higher secondary education.

After his exams were over, Ramesh arrived home, expecting Sheru to come bounding up to greet him. But got no response to his calls. Mata told him what had happened.

Shocked, Ramesh wept at having lost a loyal and dear friend without being able to say goodbye. Mata consoled him by saying that Sheru had been given to a group of Gaddis spotted camping in a nearby village. But nothing could cheer Ramesh. He wept at the thought of his childhood mate grappling with the harsh living conditions of the Gaddi tribe. He refused to eat food or talk to anyone, which disgusted and amused Babaji. Empathizing with children was considered unnecessary, and perhaps even taboo for men back then.

When Ramesh emerged from the shock, he tried to picture Sheru running free in the hills of Palampur. A smile flickered on his face, but his heart remained heavy. He never adopted a dog after that day for fear of losing it someday.

What he didn't understand is that goodbyes can't be avoided. One is destined to meet and part ways with some characters in the play of life. For Ramesh, Chota and Sheru were two such souls.

Bheenda's Little Secret

The last two decades of social media explosion have brought awareness to the fact that talent is not bound by race, gender, or class. This was very different back when Ramesh was growing up. Societal expectations rarely diverted from what one's caste offered. This story shows how breaking the shackles of tyrannous social norms such as the caste system can be done by thinking like a child.

Born into the mochi caste, Bheenda was an exceptionally bright child, but no one was aware of this. Even the schoolteachers unconsciously registered the familial background of students. If a brahmin's son could become a doctor or an engineer, a lower caste student would surpass expectations if he or she managed to pass the tenth grade.

These expectations in the classroom were mirrored on the playground. Bheenda knew it and quietly kept to his corner when the teachers returned his exceptionally written papers without a word of praise or encouragement. Things were no different at home. Plans were afoot at home to initiate Bheenda into the family trade of mending shoes as soon as he finished tenth grade. It wasn't that Bheenda's parents did not want him to do well in life, but it just didn't occur to them that their son could do more.

Bheenda's bright ways were viewed in the light of a limited future. But Bheenda had plans. Ramesh stumbled on to Bheenda's itinerary for life while out on a scouting trip with Sheru on the hillside beyond kapade.

At that time, Ramesh was in the seventh grade and Bheenda in the eighth. Sheru was the first to catch a whiff of another presence and bounded up a sloping stretch of the grassy ground. Ramesh hurried his pace when he heard an excited bark.

On the other side of the knoll sat a befuddled Bheenda, woken from his sleep by an ecstatic Sheru. Ramesh saw a carpet of papers and books surrounding Bheenda, and had no inkling how Bheenda felt about the intrusion. Bheenda's brow creased with anxiety and anger when he saw Ramesh peering into his books. But Ramesh, as curious as he was, could not bear the thought of Bheenda trying to hide something from him. For Ramesh, an attempt to hide was akin to an invitation to explore — the antidote for hundreds of loose butterflies in his tummy. Also, it compromised the sanctity of the Mangtu baba garden gang if any one member tried to keep secrets from the others. Ramesh had stood up for Bheenda's inclusion in the club when Nikku and Cheela had hesitated.

As Bheenda collected his papers, Ramesh caught a fleeting glimpse of the numbers and equations scrawled on the book Bheenda had been reading. It was a grade ten math book. 'But Bheenda is in Grade eight,' Ramesh thought as he asked Bheenda to join him and Sheru in chasing rabbits. Bheenda pursed his lips uncertainly but eventually agreed. He put his books into a worn-out cloth bag, hung it on the branch of a tree, and set off after Ramesh and Sheru.

An hour of chasing a furry gray rabbit in and out of piled up stones and around the trees siphoned the energy out of them. As they settled on the grass, Ramesh posed the question he had been burning to ask, "What were you doing with a grade ten math book?"

"Practicing," Bheenda muttered, lying on his back, eyes closed.

"Isn't it tough?"

"Not for me," Bheenda said and turned his back on Ramesh, closing his eyes. Sheru duly parked himself between the two, chewing on a thick wooden stick.

One of the many chores that Bheenda was entrusted with was herding a small cluster of four goats. It was during this time that Bheenda would hone his learning, well away from the questioning and judgmental eyes of adults, and the fracas that his younger siblings generated at home. Evenings were devoted to getting firewood and helping his mother with cooking and dishes.

Ramesh was not aware of Bheenda's circumstances. That Bheenda was an academically gifted student just never occurred to him.

Born in a fortunate milieu, great things were expected of Ramesh and his kin. But kids like Bheenda were dismissed because of their lineage. Whenever the Mangtu baba garden gang got together, Ramesh sensed the paradox of caste, ability, and expectations. Ramesh knew that Bheenda was generally bright, especially when compared to Nikku and Cheela. And those books proved he was miles ahead of his class. "I would be happy to score the highest in my own grade," Ramesh thought with a sigh.

Having risen in Ramesh's eyes as something of an expert, Bheenda was Ramesh's first choice when he found himself stuck with a math problem one day. Choti dadi could not him help with this problem, and neither could Babaji, who was too busy with legal work.

But to clear his doubts, he would have to visit Bheenda's house. He had never met Bheenda's family before. The prospect of interacting with Bheenda in the presence of his family excited him. Perhaps they were all geniuses! He set out for Bheenda's place, Sheru trotting dutifully behind him.

The mochi community lived in a crowded cluster of huts. Still, no two houses had their front doors facing each other. It was a close-set settlement of mud-brick hutments with restricted gullies for movement between them. This was remarkably different from the housing arrangement in the rest of the village. Nikku, Cheela, and Ramesh lived in individual houses surrounded by the family's farms.

The small corridor parallel to Bheenda's house was deserted at four in the afternoon. Having scanned the scene for any sign of sound or movement, Ramesh was about to turn back when he heard a moan from inside the hut on the extreme left. Ramesh moved towards the door. "Is someone there?" a raspy voice called. Sheru emitted a low growl beside him as Ramesh stepped over the threshold. He caught a slight movement and noticed a figure lying on the bed. The figure moved with slow and painful effort and inquired about Ramesh's identity. Ramesh explained that he was the headmaster's son. The trembling voice asked him to come nearer. Ramesh's eyes had grown accustomed to the dark, and now he could make out a wrinkly face that was oddly asymmetrical. One part of the face hung limply.

"I am Gopal's dadi," the soft voice said. 'Gopal,' Ramesh realized with a start, was Bheenda's real name. Bheenda had once mentioned that his dadi had been struck with paralysis. She seemed ancient, frail, and lonely. Ramesh sat on the floor mat next to her, with Sheru's head in his lap. He felt a twinge of pride in his own grandmother who even at 70 years old was spry enough to drive her daughters-in-law up the wall with her biting remarks.

He asked her where Gopal was. She explained that every Wednesday Gopal took his mother to a nearby village to visit his older brother who, dadi revealed in her scratchy voice, was 'crazy'—a term that was reserved for those with an intellectual and developmental disability back then.

Ramesh sat still as dadi went on to reveal the most intimate secrets of the family to him. From her introspective monologue punctuated with rather long intervals of silence, he gathered that Bheenda was the second born of seven children. The eldest son, Santosh, was born with a developmental disability and had been left in the care of relatives who were in touch with a good 'Ojha'—a witch doctor. Once a month, Bheenda, along with his parents, visited Santosh. Since dadi was too ill to supervise the younger kids, the neighbors pitched in to look after them.

Ramesh passed some water to Bheenda's dadi and sat chatting about goats, Mata, and the like until she dozed off. Then he silently tiptoed toward the door, his insides shaken by the cruelty of circumstances. He raced back home and went straight to his elder brother, whom he hugged long and tight before going to play with his younger sister.

Ramesh was different from other kids because he could sense others' pain. He possessed a level of empathy that was considered odd in those times. Being 'oversensitive' invited ridicule, and Ramesh was well aware of this. He was careful about expressing his feelings in the presence of others. He preferred to write them down instead.

Having seen Bheenda's plight, Ramesh now understood the quiet reserve in Bheenda. Kids rarely discuss life like philosophers. When they talk, their inner turmoil spills out as an afterthought or a dismissive statement, often self-critical—'I am so unlucky.' Adults are now beginning to acknowledge children's ability to comprehend situations, emotions, and reactions. In those days, children would simply be asked to grow up!

Ramesh never spoke to Bheenda about what he had discovered. But he did start treating Bheenda with absolute respect, something that Nikku and Cheela, in all their years of friendship, had been unable to earn. Bheenda never noticed this change because he was too busy fighting his personal battles.

One day, after Bheenda got his answer sheets for the eighth-grade exam, Ramesh asked to borrow one. Having never received a syllable of encouragement, Bheenda stoically handed his answer sheet over to Ramesh, without questions.

Ramesh gazed at the 49 out of 50 marks in math and made a beeline for Babaji's office. He handed over the sheet to Babaji, saying no student had earned such a top score before. He bet that Bheenda's marks were equally good if not better for other subjects, and that Bheenda could probably take on the tenth-grade syllabus straightaway.

Babaji, who knew Bheenda's father, was shocked by the faculty's oversight. At heart, Babaji was a teacher, and years of casteism had only affected his outer reactions. An idealist to the core, he was as proud of his son as he was happy for Bheenda.

From there, Babaji took matters in his own hands. He studied Bheenda's record and rebuked the class teacher for having dismissed the child's brilliance as a fluke. He made sure Bheenda received the proper attention, the absence of which Bheenda had hitherto taken for granted. Bheenda grew up to become a high-ranking officer as a doctor in the army.

They met but once as grown ups, as dads. Was Bheenda aware of Ramesh's role in his success? One will never know. But it didn't matter to Ramesh for he was satisfied with the thought that life could be fair and people like Bheenda had a shot at destiny.

Krishan Chacha

"You will never get married," giggled a bunch of wicked six- and seven-year-olds when they tagged Krishan's tattered kurta and ran for their lives as he turned around, feigning anger.

Krishan was the village idiot of Kamahi Devi who possessed an incredible ability to laugh at himself and weather all the personal jabs and insults with a smile.

His twinkling eyes reflected his childlike naivety. From what I can remember of our interactions during trips to the village, his eyes always instantly caught my attention.

He had happy eyes. Bubbling, giggling brooks of joyful anticipation, they belonged to a child forever expecting a gift, oblivious to the jeers and jokes of people around.

The only time I saw Krishan baba's eyes conflicted was when he was being chastised by Babaji. At that moment his eyes would flash with tiny storms in the irises. Still, I never found them sad. Perhaps his lopsided wide grin had something to do with this. The smile that stretched across the high cheekbones, a little higher on the left side of his face, remained constant in all situations. One could never tell if Krishan baba was feeling happy or blue. The only tell lay in the angle of his eyebrows and the deep dimple in his left cheek. When his brows furrowed, the dimple turned into a haggard dent on his face.

As a child, I found Krishan baba mysterious and rather frightful. At the same time, a thousand questions flooded my mind. I imagined how it might have felt to be in his shoes. If grown-ups were supposed to be mature, then how could they gang up and pick on another person? What did Krishan baba do to make everyone around him crack jokes at his expense? How could someone who laughed along with these bullies cry so easily too? And finally, how and why could anybody so readily concede to be the butt of all jokes? Why didn't he learn, or teach others a lesson? An inability to understand paradoxes as a child grows into acceptance of them as one matures. Paradoxes rarely resolve themselves, I learned later.

While on a visit to Kamahi, I heard Papa speak to Krishan baba gently about general housework—getting rations, handling farm produce, etc. "Ramesh understands me," I heard Krishan baba say many times.

Krishan baba's father was a distant relative of Ramesh's grandfather. In villages, the term 'distant relative' evokes a charming picture of rural camaraderie. If a daughter of the house settles in another village through marriage, the entire extended family becomes 'distant relatives' to her paternal and maternal families.

This relationship was enough for someone who lived in your cousin's neighborhood to drop by your house for a short or extended stay—a phenomenon lost on city dwellers, hard pressed to spend time with their own kids and siblings.

Understandably, my mother hated the idea of unannounced long-staying visitors. While on trips to the village in a rattling, ramshackle bus, I would see complete strangers walk up to my parents and greet them as if they had known them for ages. Salutations such as chachaji, mamaji, and tayaji were a staple during these visits. Except for Babaji and Mata, we hardly knew who was family and who was not.

Ramesh and his older brother treated Krishan baba like their male nanny. While some of his wicked cousins wouldn't let a chance slip by to throw a harsh comment Krishan's way, Ramesh would not poke fun at Krishan baba. It wasn't as if Ramesh was not naughty. He had his mischievous side, but he was kind to Krishan because theirs was the only family Krishan had to call his own. Krishan baba's history saddened Ramesh, and even if he cracked up at Krishan's histrionics, he couldn't bring himself to hurt him.

Ramesh and his friends called him 'chacha.' 'Chacha' literally means 'father's younger brother' but the word could be used to address any man younger than one's father. Krishan chacha performed light odd jobs around the house such as escorting the girls back safely home from school, taking the kids to somebody's house, and helping the women get firewood and carrying drinking water. In those days, having help in the kitchen was unheard of, even in the most affluent houses. All women in the family worked in the kitchen as a team—one person would get the coal and sticks burning in the chulha, and then the labor would be divided into making the dough for rotis, chopping vegetables, and getting the basics of the meal in place. The women never questioned their role as meal providers for men and children. Though Krishan chacha helped with firewood and rations, he never washed his own dishes or ate from a separate plate. His role was that of domestic help, but he was family, and everyone accepted that. He wore Babaji's old cast-off clothes and slept in the dyodhi with the rest of the men. Brand new clothes he received as gifts would be tucked away in a mysterious old suitcase under his bed, which contained many odd articles—all of them new and unspoiled, preserved carefully in their original packing.

Krishan chacha was a man with a plan from the time he had landed at Babaji's house at the age of six. He played with Babaji and his brothers as children, had seen them grow into educated members of the society and their brides light up the house with bright clothes and tinkling voices. Barely out of adolescence themselves, these girls were the first to tease Krishan about marriage. Krishan would hang around them, expecting to be asked for help with a chore, while stealing peeks at a bride's face from under the dupatta that covered her face. If watching his peers climb the ladder of life affected Krishan, no one knew. With the passing time it became apparent to everyone that marriage was not on the cards for him.

The second of three sons, Krishan was orphaned when both his parents passed away unexpectedly. His elder brother went to the nearest town to seek employment, and a close relative adopted the youngest boy. The odd-sounding and peculiar-looking Krishan presented a problem. Ramesh's grandfather, better known as Shah baba in those days, visited Krishan's house to pay his condolences and upon hearing of the family's dilemma, offered to keep the boy. This was how Krishan arrived at the threshold of their house with a bundle under his arm containing all his worldly possessions.

Krishan's elder brother grew up to own the shop where he had worked for nineteen years, because he had won the heirless owner's heart. His younger brother studied to become a lawyer in Delhi. Krishan knew nothing of all this. Denial hardened his exterior, but his soft heart hurt easily.

There would be an occasional letter from his educated brothers, which Krishan carried to almost every household in the village where someone could read. Having spread the word about his brothers' prosperity, he carried the letter to the village school where he would make a beeline for the latest teacher called masterni. In those days, female literacy in the country was less than 20 percent, and you would be hard pressed to meet a masterni. Any masterni who got posted to Kamahi became an amused recipient of Krishan's affection and doting. One way of getting the teacher's attention was bringing his brothers' letters for her to read multiple times over the years. The letters would be carefully stuffed in a plastic bag, and reread until they were crumpled beyond saving.

Wearing a loose shirt over patched and folded ankle-length pants, Krishan chacha looked like a queer fish in Babaji's old clothes since Babaji stood a foot taller than him. Krishan's quintessential asymmetrical smile completed this strange picture. He always carried a white cloth on his body sometimes flung over his shoulder at other times bundled into a crude head-gear that served multiple purposes—it could be a turban, a base to carry pots of water, or a towel to wipe away sweat.

Krishan chacha was dear to Ramesh because he seemed to belong to another world. It was a world that no one could fathom, one no other mind could access. The ease with which Krishan took all the ridicule that came his way only made him more vulnerable and precious in Ramesh's eyes. But Nikku and Cheela did not care for Krishan chacha's feelings.

Ramesh knew that chacha was a sitting duck for a cruel prank by Nikku. He looked out for Krishan and took guidance from Babaji's influence in the matter.

Children who play pranks seem diabolical, but they are just being children, busy focusing on their own desires, and blind-sighted to the possibility of hurting someone's feelings. Stopping to ponder over the results of one's actions is not a strong suit of childhood. This has to be taught, or it comes through experience, sometimes at a high cost to others.

In this case, it was Krishan chacha who bore the brunt of Nikku's penchant for creating trouble. Nikku knew he could get away with his devious plan because everyone would have a good laugh at Krishan's expense, and sleep fitfully that night, unaware of the angst a child had caused in someone. If anyone did express concern, it would be out of pity, not empathy.

Thirteen-year-old Nikku's brains were sharp, especially when it came to devising practical jokes. In Nikku's family tomfoolery was recognized and glorified as a sign of cleverness. Unfortunately, Nikku's cunning ways didn't help his academic performance, which remained modest.

In contrast, Cheela was a middling student and Ramesh was bright. Both possessed a reasonable repertoire of naughty thoughts. But while the slow-moving Cheela was an obliging pushover, Nikku was hard to dissuade once a scheme hatched in his mind. Ramesh had learned this from experience.

When Nikku suggested they write a love letter to Krishan chacha on behalf of the new masterni at school, Ramesh shot down the idea right away. But Nikku was already beholden to the humor of this scheme. Shooting Ramesh a wary glance, Nikku motioned to Cheela, who bade Ramesh goodbye and followed Nikku.

Ramesh, still suspicious of Nikku, dawdled on his way back home, tapping the stones with a thin wooden stick he had carried to scare away any nasty insects or reptiles driven to land by the heavy rains.

Nikku and Cheela went straight to Nikku's elder brother, Naresh, and let him in on the prank, bubbling with laughter.

Naresh shook his head in amusement but acquiesced, and together they jotted down a billet-doux with the mushiest words possible. Nikku snatched the missive from Naresh's hands and ran with Cheela to find Krishan.

They found him sitting under the Peepal tree by the Toba. "Krishan chacha, masterni has sent this letter for you," Nikku said, out of breath and poker-faced. Krishan's eyes lit up. He could not read, so he asked Nikku to read it to him. Finding it difficult to control the tsunami of laughter rising inside of him, Nikku started reading.

"My dearest darling Krishan." The salutation was enough to send that grin on chacha's face into a tizzy. He sat down on his haunches as he listened to the masterni pour out her heart in Nikku's childish and high-pitched voice.

"I told you I would get the best bride in the village," chacha said when Nikku finished reading the letter. A renewed confidence and crispness infused his being as he snatched the letter out of Nikku's hand and started for the village to tell anyone and everyone of this development.

The first ones to read the letter were the brides of the house. Knowing well enough that a teacher could never fall for the dim-witted Krishan, they immediately understood that someone had played a prank on him. Meanwhile, Krishan chacha changed into a new shirt and pants from the trunk under his bed, items which had been saved for such an occasion. His first stop would be outside the quarters of the brides. He would bask in the adoration of dumbstruck women of the household. The usually gawky and untidy Krishan emerged in flashy attire only to be greeted by hysterical laughter from the women. When he asked them to lend him a mirror, Guddi bua said, "Chacha, masterni won't marry you. Don't go to the school."

But chacha was intent on meeting the teacher in his best-groomed form. During all of this, in the grip of indolence that only a summer afternoon could cause, Ramesh was sound asleep. Chacha knew that even though it was holiday time, the teaching staff would still be at school for paper-checking and other administrative work.

Unaffected by the taunting women, Krishan stumbled out on towards the school, mumbling to himself, marveling at his luck—his heart both refused to believe in the meeting and feared it would happen.

The lady teacher at the village school was married and tolerant of the jokes going around about her and Krishan because she realized it was a tradition of sorts. Other women had gone through this before. It took her an hour to travel to the village each day, and acceptance by the students of a new school was always a challenge. Playing along had helped her quickly settle down as a teacher, but she hoped to get transferred to a school nearer to her home soon.

On this fateful day, Santosh the masterni was in a hurry to finish work and catch the last bus home. If she didn't do that, she would have to wait for a tonga to leave for her village. As she hurried with her paper checking, she saw Krishan shuffling towards her, looking excited and shy. Without a word, avoiding her eye like a blushing bride, he handed the letter to the male teacher sitting next to Santosh the masterni. The math teacher read the missive and passed it to Santosh, his expression as blank as the summer sky.

Puzzled, Santosh took the letter. Even a few kilometers of distance between villages made people appear strange and alien, and Kamahi Devi had surpassed her expectations in this regard. She was tempted to put aside the letter and finish checking the last few exam papers, but when she saw the salutation at the beginning of the letter, she dropped the pen she held in her hand.

She got up in a rage as she read the letter and rushed to Babaji's office. She handed the note to Babaji and started weeping, expressing her fears about her reputation being at stake, now that another teacher had also read the letter.

Meanwhile, a confused Krishan stood outside waiting.

When Babaji stepped out, Krishan tried to present his confident side, straightening his shirt and pressing down his hair. Babaji strode towards him and slapped his face.

Even though he was reduced to tears, Krishan chacha refused to tell Babaji who had given him the letter. Babaji knew that Krishan could not write, but with the entire village making merry at Krishan's cost, it would be hard to pin down the culprit unless Krishan helped.

With his arms wrapped around his head, Krishan rocked on his haunches and wept out the agony accumulated over years of humiliation and desperation. Babaji, touched by his plight, exhorted Krishan to tell him who had played the prank on him. But he failed to get any answers. Babaji changed his tactic and took to chastising chacha for stepping out of line, for coveting someone beyond his reach. Krishan chacha kept mum, staring at a point on the floor through teary eyes.

As the news spread, Krishan chacha disappeared like he always did when Babaji berated him. Ramesh didn't know of this until four days later when he couldn't find Krishan anywhere. A reluctant Cheela narrated the whole incident to Ramesh while giggling but quietened when Ramesh glared and walked away. Ramesh knew why Krishan chacha had not spilled the beans on Nikku and Cheela. "He must have thought I would be in on this with them," Ramesh muttered, as guilt washed over him. He rushed to tell Babaji the complete story.

That evening Babaji visited the families of Nikku and Cheela, and after a friendly banter with their fathers, he told Nikku and Cheela they would spend their break time cleaning up the school's animal shed for a month after the school opened.

In those days punishments consisted of a good caning, manual work around the school, or squatting in the class's corner as a murga—a form of corporal punishment where the person must loop his arms behind his knees to grip his ears. While Nikku and Cheela escaped the caning, in addition to cleaning the barn they were made to sit as murgas through the entire length of the school assembly for a month.

After this incident, Krishan chacha kept a safe distance from the school masternis, though secretly he never gave up on his ambition to one day marry a schoolteacher. Nikku continued to tease chacha about his bachelor status. Santosh masterni forgave chacha.

And Papa realized that in Krishan chacha he had a friend and ally for a lifetime.

For the Love of Mata!

Papa and I had one thing in common—we were both fond of Mata. That Mata loved all her kids and grandkids comes as no surprise; all grandparents love to behold, occasionally tease, and indulge their grandchildren. Nevertheless, according to many, Mata herself was not a very lovable person.

There was an oddity about Mata—a certain self-centeredness that I feel helped her live into her late nineties.

Living is like a boxing match—between a person and life itself. Infancy is learning to survive, schooling is learning to don your gear for the fight—the helmet, the gloves, the mouth guard, etc. The first decade of adulthood is the time to practice what you've learned so far. One responds to life's pummeling with counter punches, and sometimes even life stands back and applauds.

But while the spirit and gusto of life might remain intact, when a person eventually starts to give in to the hard-knocks, life moves in with a final blow crushing its adversary. If ever there was a worthy opponent for the champion in this boxing match, it was Mata. An unabashed zest for life and a complete belief in her own actions made up her defenses.

First, I must touch upon what made Mata who she was—a devoted wife and loving mother (especially to her sons and grandsons). She was the prototype of 'woman is the enemy of woman.' Save for her daughter, she spared no other woman from pointing out flaws and indulging in one-upmanship. And through all this, she held on to a firm belief that God was her ally—and he better be, considering the hours she spent fasting, praying, and making offerings. In a pinch, anyone who chose to have a showdown with Mata had better know what they signed up for.

As she aged, people around her resigned themselves to her ways, and their anger gave way to annoyance and dislike. But Mata was not one to relent. How could she give up being herself? She remained fiercely independent and as biting in her remarks as ever. She never got rid of her critical eye.

In her mind, there was always a good reason for her petty actions and hurtful words. To her credit, Mata never kept grudges for more than a day, and rarely wished bad fortune for anyone. Her hardheadedness was transparent—this flaw was there for all to see. Also, there was no desire in her to be liked by others. But those treated to her spite-filled words and actions rarely forgot them.

How did Mata earn mine and Papa's fondness? Looking back, I figured that we both overlooked the quirks in her behavior and simply discarded them as one might peel away layers of a musty, discolored onion to discover the fresh, healthy and soft interior. This revealed an endearing side of her. In this light, her unnecessary wickedness seemed like a child's mischief. Her tendency to make fun of others made her unique, rather than vicious, at her age. Yes, Mata could entertain you with mimicry and parodies that surfaced as funny asides. Others saw Mata in the limited scope of their egos. We found it difficult to separate her from our own flaws. It took two highly sentimental people to understand and forgive Mata's paltry machinations. In this light everything she did was pardonable.

We could disapprove of Mata's behavior, feel angry at her schemes, and giggle at her quirkiness. That she was aware of this bond was clear. When she visited us, she rarely approached my brother or my sister if she wanted a chore such as posting a letter or putting a snack together done. She straightaway came to me.

I fell for Mata's toothless grin, trivial scheming, comic imitations, and her gutsy competition with other grandmas and her own daughters-in-law. Papa was so attuned to his parents' needs that they rarely had to ask him for anything because he anticipated these. He was blind to Mata's faults. When the rest of the family including Babaji shook their heads dismissively at Mata's actions, Papa accepted them with an amused detachment. Nothing Mata did could make Papa angry. This was also why Papa was Mata's favorite and Mom the most criticized daughter-in-law.

I penned this fictionalized incident to draw a character sketch of Mata. To those who feel I have been harsh, I apologize. Considering my attachment to Mata, those who knew her well may find it an inaccurate and exonerating account. Let us therefore take the spotlight away from Mata. Let it instead be seen as an exposé on how children come to discover their parents as flawed and human.

Nowadays, children judge their parents more than they did when I was little. The same was unthinkable in Ramesh's childhood. However, unlike most children, Ramesh loved to ruminate. Therefore, most people around, excluding Babaji, were scrutinized by him. Ramesh had the habit of making light of 'character flaws' in others. He liked to see people in a humorous vein, and rarely forgot his initial impressions. As a father, he candidly stated his views about the company we kept, but never forced us give up any friendships. For this reason, I gave consideration to his opinion even if I pretended otherwise.

It was no different with Mata. She was his mother, and a kind person at heart. All mothers grumbled, smothered their kids, and shielded them from the wrath of their fathers.

It once came to pass that Babaji, after selling a piece of land, decided to bump up his contribution to the wedding of his younger brother's daughter. In a joint family, a daughter's wedding was usually a joint affair. In their house, Babaji and his four brothers all pitched in. In those days, weddings were uncomplicated affairs. Community meals were the most significant component of the celebrations. The jewelry gifted to the bride, though important, was limited to essential and functional pieces.

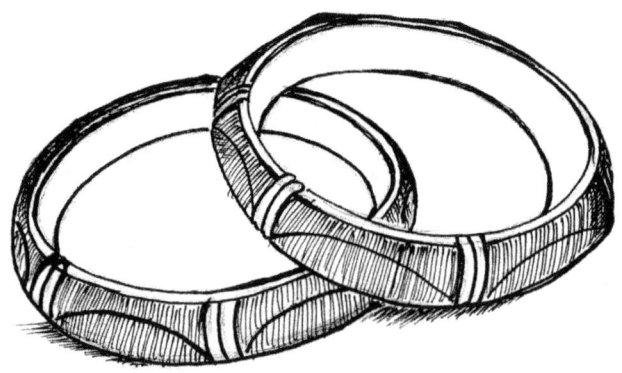

This time, however, Babaji felt like chipping in more because the family that the girl was to be married into lived in a developed town with amenities the villagers didn't have. So, during a trip to Talwada, Babaji bought a pair of thick gold bracelets for the bride. Ramesh sat flipping through a book in Mata's room when Babaji entered and handed over the bracelets to Mata.

Now Mata, true to her nature, was protective of her own brood. She could not justify the thought of another daughter of the house receiving more than her own daughter. But she knew her logic would not hold water with Babaji. Without a word, she tucked away the pouch of bangles in the large wooden trunk that sat at the foot of her rope-mesh bed inside her bedroom. Covered with a heavy hand-woven rug, this trunk was a treasure house where Mata stashed away everything—from jewelry to dry fruits to fancy cutlery. Fine clothing and velvets that came later as the dowry for her daughters-in-law and treats like pinnis, pedas, and aamla-murrabba were all placed under the protection of the heavy lid of the chest and secured with a thick iron latch.

More than once, along with my kid brother and sister, I raided the trunk after swiping the keys hidden under Mata's pillow, in search of those tasty treats. Mata's trunk held a mystical fascination for us. The diversity of contents we chanced upon—pretty, fragile, or delicious—was enough to make exploring the trunk our mission on lazy summer afternoons or foggy winter evenings. By the time my five-year-old daughter visited the village house and met Mata, who was by then in her eighties, the trunks had increased in number from one to three.

Rummaging through jars and hiding places holds an unspeakable charm. I have yet to come across any child who hasn't explored the out-of-bounds food shelf on the sly or poked about in the refrigerator looking for yummies.

As grown-ups, we keep in touch with the child in us by raiding the pantry once in a while. This may not be true for everyone, but it's definitely a worthwhile caper.

Getting back to the story about the bangles—it just so happened that as soon as Mata placed the bangles in the trunk, right next to a jar of almond khatais, was when Dabbo, a featherbrained daughter of Babaji's younger brother, walked into the room asking Mata for new cups and saucers to serve tea to some guests who had just arrived. Mata hastily shut the trunk. Ramesh, who had been lazing on a manji nearby, got up to get a good look out the window at the people who planned to take one of his sisters away.

Having ensured that Mata had safely placed the bangles in the trunk, Babaji exited the room. Mata looked at Dabbo sharply. Handing her trunk's keys to Dabbo, Mata instructed her to get the cups and saucers and hurried after Babaji to hand him his starch-stiff white turban. Dabbo rummaged through the chest for cutlery and, when she couldn't find any, joined Ramesh at the window for a peek at the guests. Before long she remembered the ongoing preparations for tea and hurried out, leaving the trunk's lid open. Ramesh dragged himself back to the bed and fell asleep. Later, when Mata returned to her room to find the trunk open, she made a hue and cry about Dabbo's lack of wits. Everybody agreed, including Babaji, that Dabbo should not have been given the keys.

This was the opportunity that Mata had been looking for. That evening, as Babaji was leaving the kitchen, Mata called him aside and coolly informed him that one of the gold bangles had gone missing. Anger mingled with confusion as Babaji debated whether he should break the news to the rest of the family. This might even result in suggesting Dabbo had taken the ornament. Even though he doubted that Dabbo, who was all innocence and naivety, could ever do such a thing. But any child might be attracted to a piece of jewelry.

With the house overflowing with guests, confronting Dabbo meant potential conflict. After much thought, as Mata had foreseen, Babaji decided to let the matter rest for the moment. The next day, while Babaji was relaxing in the afternoon, he told Ramesh's elder brother to question Dabbo playfully about the bangle. Babaji sighed, "Your Mata is sure." Ramesh overhead all of this.

"A theft at the time I was sleeping in the room!" thought Ramesh as he made his way to Mata's room, which he treasured for its cool shaded interiors and sleep-inducing ambiance. As he entered, he saw Mata inspecting a pair of bangles that she quickly stowed away when she heard him at the door. Ramesh, now 14 years old, suddenly understood the whole ploy.

More importantly, he suddenly saw Mata as a thief—a greedy gold loving lady, very unlike his mother. In fact, the sight of Mata with the bangles she had herself declared as stolen severed the imaginary umbilical cord that keeps a child attached to a parent with reverence.

Here she was, just another individual like any other. She might as well have been a hog like Nikku's chachi or as rude as Cheela's mother. At that moment, he wondered if all mothers in the world were better than his own. Ramesh suddenly felt the need for something positive about his mother to hang to.

Meanwhile, oblivious to Ramesh's turmoil, Mata fussed about him and told him how tired he looked—"Working your fingers to the bone for wedding work and having to study hard at the same time." She fluffed up the mattress and the pillow and then patted Ramesh to sleep. As she lovingly pushed Ramesh's hair off his forehead, deep in her own thoughts, Ramesh understood that the love of a parent is unconditional. And sometimes this can cloud their better sense.

He suddenly thought of all the tight spots that he, Nikku, and Cheela had landed themselves in, and how Mata had saved him by shielding him from Babaji. Babaji would rant and fume, and Mata weathered the tirade, confident in her child's innocence.

Ramesh drifted off to sleep with these thoughts and woke up with a start when he heard Babaji ask Mata if she had found the bangle. Mata glanced at Ramesh and answered, "Valuable jewelry once lost is gone forever." Ramesh pretended to sleep and decided that the matter was between Babaji and Mata. Years later, he discovered that Mata had gifted the bangles to his sister at the birth of her first child.

Mata's absence of guilt and the irreproachable rationale for her actions confused Ramesh. Is another person's conviction enough to convince you about the correctness of an action? For Ramesh, who went on to study law, the experience was formative. Whenever he had to present a case in court, he made it a point to look thoroughly convinced himself, regardless of the evidence in hand. Ramesh became Mata, and his client, who had put his faith in Ramesh by hiring him, became his child.

You might call it a twisted lesson in parenting. I see it as a child's acceptance of a parent's flaws. When it came to mothering, Mata came out on top for Papa.

Circuit House

A love for wandering had surfaced early in Ramesh's life. It began on his journey back home, alone on the bus from bua's house, when he was thirteen.

At one point on the route, called Cheer Dee Khui, only one road winds through the landscape like a thread stringing together some fifty odd villages on both sides of this road. On my trips to the village as a child, I remember trying to memorize every bus stop through minute differences in the landscape.

It turned out to be an exercise in splitting hairs. Still, I remembered a few villages' names by landmarks such as a tea-shack, a shop, or a temple by the roadside. The other villages had either grassy flat surfaces with a cement milestone painted white for marking the bus stop, or a rubble-filled expanse of white stones that the bus couldn't have possibly crossed. Narrow trails or dirt tracks led away from the road to villages located beyond the hills and clusters of trees. I remember gazing from the window of the bus, towards the concealed villages, and imagining life there.

Sometimes I would use my forefinger to trace out a path that led to the corner of a house peeking through the distant trees. Without gadgets, bus journeys were a daze of boredom caused by the movement of the bus and the palpable silence of the passengers. My attention would move outside the window to the landscape flying by. My flights of fancy regarding the lives and characters in other village communities would add thrill and anticipation to the journey. Were there more kids like us who lived in big cities and visited their grandparents in the villages every year? Did these kids also forget their day-to-day worries about school and playground politics back home in the city and give into the abandon of childhood in a village for a few days?

As Ramesh sat in the bus, he felt lucky to be part of the post-independence generation. There were visible signs of development that a villager appreciated differently. Tongas were history and buses now plied frequently between Daulatpur and the road that had sprung from Cheer Dee Khui.

This particular day, Ramesh was sleepy and tired, having stayed up half the night perfecting his game of marbles and Carom Board with Nandi and Bholu. But he wanted to enjoy his ride back home sitting shotgun with the bus driver. The lone seat kept accidental, swaying and bold sleepers away. For it was the unspoken natural right of travelers in public transport—'when sleepy or nauseous, thy neighbor's shoulder is thy rightful prop.' The view of the road rushing beneath the bus was meditative. The ride had begun with the driver chatting nineteen to the dozen, and in spite of the rule never to sleep in the passenger seat, the driver indulgently and protectively let Ramesh slip into slumber.

Thus, deep in sleep, Ramesh awoke with a start when he heard the conductor bellow, "Banauli." He had never heard that name before. "I must have crossed Kamahi," he muttered and stepped off the bus. He was well-acquainted with the villages around Kamahi, so to find himself in an unknown village meant he had overshot his village by many stops. But Ramesh could not bring himself to ask the driver for directions.

Ramesh was at an age when admitting a mistake was unthinkable. He would rather brave the odds than give others a chance to ridicule him. He hated it when someone condoned his behavior by saying, "He's just a boy!" It was fortunate that he had started the journey early that morning and had the entire day to find his way back home.

Ramesh turned back on the road from Banauli, looking for familiar sights, hill formations, temples, and faces. This accidental trek opened his eyes to the wealth of nature surrounding his own village. In those days, paranoia about kids getting lost or kidnapped or abused was non-existent. The countrymen and women, having lived through colonial slavery, were blinded by the shiny possibilities and idealism of a free nation.

Parents were a lot calmer back then. Still, alarm bells went off for Krishan chacha when Ramesh did not get off the bus at the scheduled hour. He lingered for a while, and trooped back home with a long face. The family fumed and waited for Ramesh to get home. But Ramesh, oblivious to his parents' turmoil got busy discovering the joys of a footloose life.

On his way back, Ramesh saw bevies of young girls with water-filled gaggars (enormous brass pots) braced on their heads, managing the feat of chattering and balancing the heavyweight containers at the same time. A few of them catcalled his way. He hurried on, smiling to himself.

He saw children younger than him herding buffaloes to a Toba, and one odd kid comfortably sitting astride a buffalo. He saw farmers in fields with the womenfolk looking like swarthy Arabs—with tightly tied dupattas that covered half of their foreheads. Here and there, a stranger would ask him where he was from and upon hearing the name Kamahi, would amicably remark that he had heard of masterji.

There were those who had never heard of masterji before, and it was these people who helped Ramesh see that there was a world beyond Babaji, Kamahi, Phuphaji, and Daulatpur. A world waiting to be discovered and made his own.

He reached home just as daylight was fading over the distant hills. He found Mata in a grumbling fit and a defensive Babaji doing his best to allay her anxiety. No one thought of scolding Ramesh when they saw him, so great was their relief. After a quick hug and a close look to make sure he was all right, Mata made a beeline for her personal deity's shrine to fulfill the first of the long list of promises she had made to God as she implored him to look after Ramesh and get him home safe and sound.

This was how Ramesh discovered his stroll-happy wanderlust.

When we went on family vacations, Papa would leave the party immediately to explore the surroundings, while the rest of the family gave in to travel fatigue and tickled our taste buds with steaming cups of tea and a plate of pakoras. By the time we got ready for a travel-induced snooze, he would be back with an itinerary and information about all the tourist hotspots.

When Papa told me how he had discovered the mysterious Circuit House, I was hardly surprised. Indeed, the movie Mahal, a murder mystery which starred the 1950s actress, Madhubala, was but a prequel to what Papa had in mind—a spooky plot set in the Circuit House.

Ramesh belonged to the generation that had missed India's independence by a hair's breadth. Born in 1948, his infancy and childhood held only a fading whiff of the euphoria of newfound freedom. And ample access to British literature was enough to produce boundless curiosity about the angrez in kids. That generation was probably more smitten by the British lifestyle than the one that came before it. In fact, Ramesh, in keeping with the expectations set by him, duly pursued a Masters in Law, but his real passion lay in the fictional worlds and romantic backdrops created by Charles Dickens, Shakespeare, Chaucer, Percy B. Shelley, and William Wordsworth.

Without any intention to commit an apostasy, but much to Mata's horror all the same, Ramesh had compiled a large list of psalms and sayings selected from the Bible and British poets' religious works, which Mata believed was the phirangi's way of casting a spell on Indian kids to lead them away from their native land. Come to think of it, I always got a feeling that Papa was a closet atheist. His confusion regarding religion could be partly attributed to the two highly contrasting worlds he was exposed to—one through his quotidian life, and the other, through books and literature.

One world, which was non-literary and conventional, consisted of parents and family. Superstition was rampant, and women were still largely uneducated and wore a ghoonghat or a veil over their faces. In this world, rituals defined one's entire life. In contrast, the other world he was exposed to was governed by scientific inquiry and progress. He liked the idea of choice especially in matters of belief.

Perhaps being untouched by the ugly reality of racial discrimination and losing touch with his roots—which also included stories about his benevolent grandfather, Shah Baba—further contributed to Ramesh's alienation from his own family's way of life.

In those days the most prominent symbol of British Raj, especially in the rural quarters, was Babudom. Official dignitaries were often treated like kings and queens. Their residence, the local Circuit House, was the largest and most well-kept house in town—a mini palace with heavy silk draperies and upholsteries, silver cutlery, every inch of floor carpeted, and everything maintained by an army of domestics.

The spontaneous association between Circuit House and the angrez had Ramesh's imagination working overtime, fueled by stories of lost love, ghosts, and betrayals at the mysterious Circuit House. The Circuit House in question is located a little distance before Palampur, in the village of Dadhi. The word literally means 'beard' in Hindi, and had prompted many a bearded man to jump when the bus conductor announced that people from Dadhi should prepare to disembark.

I know of the Circuit House and Papa's dream because he shared it with us. He loved to visit the places where he had grown up—his school, college, university, and various locations where he had worked. I suspect he believed that by including us in these experiences, he could preserve these moments of his life.

Perhaps it was his way of holding on to his youth and childhood. After all, it is only when one turns into a parent that reality hits—a particular phase of life is over, and all cherished experiences can now safely be stored as 'memories.' But most parents don't realize that narrating their life experiences to children makes parents seem more ancient than ever!

On one such jaunt to Dharamshala, the hill town where Papa had first started practicing law, he showed us an ominous-looking solitary house with a pitched roof, a front deck, and decent-sized windows. The building was clearly visible from the main road. It spanned a grassy hillside along the road that led into the town. Opposite the house, across the street, we could see scattered shops and fruit carts, which tempted travelers with their fresh and colorful wares before they entered the hustle and bustle of the central town. Papa parked the car next to a cart selling apples, and herded us towards the Circuit House. While my younger brother and sister were away in hostels, Mom and I were deep in discussion about where to stop for lunch. Eyeing the juicy fruits, Mom moved toward the carts, and I was glad to stretch my limbs.

I surveyed the old wooden structure of the Circuit House that stood in ruins. I could tell that it stirred something in Papa, so I fell into step with him. I realized that we could never see the building the same way as Papa did. It was a part of his world, not mine. As an adult, I understand that some dreams are essential just for being dreams—the soft cotton clouds that support the world-weary spirit that carries the burden of social and familial expectations as one grows older.

As Papa gazed lovingly at the structure, he said, "I've always wanted to direct a movie set in that Circuit House." With these words, he passed his dream to us. And even though penning the following story is nothing like directing a movie, in the frenzied alleys of my mind, I see him as a teenager visiting the Circuit House, his hair as slick as that of an English babu.

Ramesh first chanced upon the Circuit House on one of his trips with Babaji for a land deal in a village near Dharamshala. This was after he had been sent to Talwada for high school, and was visiting home during the holidays. Those days, kids could afford to wander and be spontaneously adventurous, unlike the curated adventures for kids nowadays. After all, everyone knew someone in every village in the region! Ramesh had gotten into the habit of trekking off to new hamlets. At these spots, he liked to be a fly on the wall, though an occasional howdy-do in the form of "masterji's boy!" was not wholly unwelcome. He would finish his excursions by the time Babaji was done with his business.

A forget-me-not blue sky promised a day full of adventure for 14-year-old Ramesh as he set off to discover the village on his own while Babaji was busy discussing the prices of land, mango trees, and the recently established and ineffective Panchayat policies. Ramesh's solid brown fabric pants and plain white shirt, which had been carefully selected by Mata for such an occasion, made him stand out from the rest of the village crowd. Despite his worn-out though sturdy leather shoes and wild curly hair Ramesh looked like an urbanite, a townie in love with hills.

He hummed a Pahari song—hariye ni pariye, subz khajure, patru jina de pile ho—as he walked with a light step, a stick in his hand which was another dead giveaway of his village upbringing. He planned to head straight for the central market to look for the popular watering hole for the village folk—Bholaram's Mithai shop.

Every village in those days had a mithai shop that prepared a unique sweet treat. It would never be the same elsewhere because it carried the cook's unique influence. Differentiating these through ingredients was a superfluous exercise, for these sweets were mostly concoctions of wheat, condensed milk, cottage cheese, ghee, and sugar. Kamahi, for example, was famous for its milk pedas.

Ramesh noticed a cluster of shops and made a beeline for the one with a huge halwai's wok poking out into the street. A creaky, faded sign next to the shack announced it was Bholaram's Mithai shop.

He had heard that Jalebi was the famous mithai in this village, and Ramesh gave it his stamp of approval when he bit into syrupy jalebis, which he paired with a glass of hot milk. As Bholaram fished out concentric rings of fried batter from a pool of boiling hot ghee and dunked these in sugar syrup, he chatted with Ramesh, a flimsy hand towel flung over his shoulder to wipe his hands on.

Ramesh learned that a nautanki or a street play was being staged in the village that weekend, and that a local lad had made a name for himself by being the first to enter graduate college in Chandigarh. He learned that the residents were a proud lot, for the English had considered their little hamlet important enough to construct a Circuit House there. He observed and noted the patchwork of people that made up the village—their dreams, aspirations, attitudes, and humility.

As he did this, he came to see Dadhi as a special place. "No one thought of constructing a Circuit House in Kamahi," he thought. The bent-over halwai narrated the various milestones that made Dadhi a remarkable village, while focusing on outlining perfect little spirals of batter that trickled through a bunched up muslin cloth into hot bubbling ghee.

The slightly nippy October air blew into the halwai's shack and streamed out through the back window. A straw windowpane hung on for dear life by a crude single-nailed hinge at the back window.

There were few visitors to the shack during the early morning, but as the day wore on, the marketplace would buzz with chatter. Bholaram provided directions to the Circuit House to Ramesh and also packed 100 grams of jalebis on the house for the child to eat later in the day. As Ramesh walked purposefully toward his destination, he observed a group of youngsters playing gulli-danda in the mellow morning sun. But he did not feel tempted to join them. When he wanted to, he could easily leave the rest of the world behind, and concentrate on a chosen task. He hummed a Pahari tune, and listened to leaves stir restlessly as the playful breeze twirled them around. He dug into the jalebis and mulled over his chat with the halwai. "The Circuit House is said to be haunted," the halwai had told him.

Mystery was in the air as he arrived at the Circuit House, a bright whitewashed building that had an aloof, hoity-toity look. With no government official visiting at that moment, the deserted Circuit House stood invitingly, bursting with intrigue and untold stories.

Ramesh stepped onto the wooden steps, his hand reassuringly skimming the railing. He climbed onto the deck which must have served as a porch for afternoon tea ceremonies for the English babus. The silence unnerved him. He felt his heart lurch when he heard a sound behind him and grabbed the balustrade which lined the front edge of the porch. An old man stood a few paces from Ramesh.

"Why are you snooping around, young man?"

Ramesh told him he was a visitor from out of town, and that he liked to write and wanted to know everything about the Circuit House and its past occupants. Dhenu chacha, as he was called by the villagers, grinned from ear to ear, for he had found an audience for the tales he loved to share. It was an audience he rarely received.

Dhenu chacha belonged to the imaginative league that Ramesh was unknowingly a part of. Tales of fairies or war-tormented lands, of love lost or tarnished, of betrayals or undying loyalty… all provided a fascinating respite from the everyday drudgery of their creed. While Ramesh would go on to read established authors and works of English literature, Dhenu chacha had to seize every opportunity to express his creative steam by spinning tales about people he had met at the Circuit House. As a storyteller, I can say that he was justified in doing so.

Dhenu chacha had witnessed the transition of power from an enslaved to an independent India. A spot relatively untouched by the political goings-on, ever since the gora sahibs had stopped visiting, Dadhi had remained deserted except recently when an Indian babu had arrived, poor-mouthing everything in sight. The babu acted like he was a gora sahib. His affected behavior made Dhenu chacha wonder if independence really meant anything if there was no change in the attitudes of the upper echelons towards the poor and the illiterate. For all purposes, Dhenu chacha's subservient station in life remained unchanged. "This is probably why civil servants are still revered and mollycoddled by the masses," Papa observed years later.

"There lived here a gora couple who possessed the beauty of Ram and Sita," Dhenu chacha began.

"Ram and Sita?" Ramesh asked doubtfully.

"Do you want to hear the story or not?" Dhenu chacha spat at him. Ramesh nodded in apology.

"They were called the Smiths."

Ramesh fingered the old paneled wooden doors as Dhenu chacha dipped into his vast reservoir of memories to select a fascinating story, thus sowing the seeds of a movie plot in Ramesh's mind.

In the decade following 1910, Dhenu, a 15-year-old, was recruited as a gardener at the Circuit House. The Circuit House then was not as lavish as it would eventually become. A few years after Ramesh's visit, it would serve as a sophisticated reminder of British rule, thanks to repair work and whimsical makeovers by the Indian babus. Still, when Dhenu joined, it was pretty and sprawling, and Dhenu made sure not a leaf went uncared for in the manicured lawns.

At 15, Dhenu was an enthusiastic mali, or gardener, eager to learn, with no other dreams other than to be a mute servant to the gora sahibs.

That February had been unusually cold. While it generally snowed in the upper reaches of Mcleodganj, snow rarely ever reached Dadhi. Typically, early signs of spring appeared in February, but that year snow still covered Dadhi with a milky white blanket.

As young Dhenu sat on his haunches, his head draped in a woolen scarf, he scraped the barren patches of lawn with his fingertips to determine if the soil was still hard, or if it was time to plant fresh grass in the garden. He heard raised voices coming from within the house. He moved towards the window of the living room for a quick peek. "The British officer who had moved five months before with his beautiful wife sat in his plush velvet chair puffing on a tobacco pipe, while the lady stumbled from one corner of the room to another as if she were walking on smoldering embers and wanted to kill someone for it," Dhenu said.

Ramesh took a pause from visualizing the scene to admire Dhenu chacha's gift for dramatics.

"Her eyes were bloodshot, and her curly hair lay unkempt on her shoulders. She kept glaring at the sahib as if she would kill him. I climbed the ledge of an adjacent window for a better view. I was fearless back then," Dhenu recounted. Ramesh settled himself on the wooden staircase, absorbed in watching the Munchausen in Dhenu emerge.

In pre-independent India, peaceful villages in this part of the world put the sahibs on pedestals. They were not aware of world trade issues, salt marches, or political dramas unfolding elsewhere in the country. But social niceties still defined a person, so when the sahib took memsahib in his arms, Dhenu quickly withdrew from the window lest they should discover him eavesdropping. Similar scenes with a cool-as-cucumber sahib and an angry, distraught memsahib repeated themselves over the next month, and the shouting slowly increased in intensity. Dhenu heard the cook and other servants of the house whisper amongst themselves, but no one thought of Dhenu as grown up enough to discuss anything going on around him. When the lady of the house approached him one day with a bewitching smile, he could only nod, acutely aware of his hammering heart.

"What's your name?" the lady asked in broken Hindi to Dhenu, her words sounded like the tinkling of the delicate silver bells that still adorned the massive Christmas tree in the living room. "Dhenu," the paralyzed child replied.

Dhenu could not bring himself to look directly into her eyes. He had often peeped through the garden window long enough to gaze at the soft, creamy tone of the lady's skin, and hair that reflected the warm yellow of the farms in the month of Baisakh.

"Will you do something for me?" she asked. Dhenu looked up shyly, surprised by the question. How could the lady who had all that she wanted, including grown-up servants to do her bidding, wish anything of him?

Dhenu looked up and was dazzled by desperate hazel eyes piercing his own. "Yes, memsahib," Dhenu croaked in Hindi, somewhat scared by his own voice, still staring wide-eyed at her face, expecting to receive a slap for his audacity.

"Dhenu, can you take me to sadhu baba?" the lady whispered.

"Sadhu baba? The one who lives on the teela?" Dhenu asked, thrown off by this request. Sadhu baba was a notorious tantrik who lived on top of a hill about two kilometers outside the village. One could see his pitched tent and ragged pennant flag from afar. Though renowned for his mystical powers and acumen in black magic, for Dhenu the sadhu baba represented someone who fed on others' fears. Only the most desperate souls, the ones who had given up hope, sought him out.

Sharp-tongued mothers-in-law dragged young brides who could not conceive to baba, to be handed over for 'treatment.' Women sought amulets to bewitch a married man, to steal somebody else's luck, or to avenge personal grievances. All of sadhu baba's dealings had a shade of noir to them, and Dhenu's own mother disapproved profoundly of such practices.

Dhenu was suddenly scared. He understood that a request to meet sadhu baba meant the situation between the couple was dire.

"Will you take me to him?" the memsahib asked again.

"All right," Dhenu said, nodding. He struck the trowel deep into the earth to extirpate a weed as the lady walked back to the house.

The next evening, Dhenu quietly took to snipping the hedge near the same spot where the memsahib, called Margaret, had cornered him the day before. He heard a sound behind him and saw Banto, memsahib's parlor maid, beckoning to him.

"She's calling you," Banto said, glancing around and giving Dhenu a questioning look. Banto was herself twenty-one years old and completely enamored by the lifestyle of angrezi people.

The two of them silently made it to the lady's room. Once inside, Dhenu began to tremble. The warm fire blazing in the fireplace did nothing to calm his nerves. Margaret stood staring into the fire.

"Did you contact sadhu baba?" the memsahib asked after a few moments of awkward silence. She moved towards him and held out some coins. Banto elbowed Dhenu, who held up his hand. It felt like begging. He had carried out Margaret's order out of duty, not for money. Margaret dropped some paisa in his hand without a hint of recognition or a smile. At this moment, Dhenu felt really small. With great difficulty he found his voice.

'Tomorrow at three,' Dhenu said in Hindi, showing the time by sticking out three fingers. He felt the blush of embarrassment and shame on his face.

"Good," Margaret said. "You will take us there then."

As Dhenu stepped out of the house, he suddenly felt very grown-up and mature. Who would have thought he would enter the bedroom of a British lady, aid in her secret maneuverings, and be relied upon by her for the completion of a clandestine project!

The next day, a much more confident Dhenu, dressed in his best, met the ladies—Margaret and Banto—in the expansive backyard of the Circuit House. Together they slid out through the roughly hewn wooden back gate.

They trudged their way to the tent, choosing hidden trails over the ones visible from the hillside. Margaret spent about thirty minutes in sadhu baba's tent while Dhenu waited outside with a preoccupied and perturbed Banto. Finally Margaret came out unhurried and as poker-faced as usual—she didn't betray a hint of what had transpired inside or what she was feeling.

Dhenu marveled at how adept the angrez were at keeping a straight face. His mother's face would have told a thousand stories by now, with a sprinkling of melodrama and a dash of pretend bravura. Dhenu noticed that Margaret carried what looked like a taveej, or amulet, in her hand. As they hurried down the hilltop, no one spoke, and once near the house, the lady almost ran inside the gate without so much as a glance or a word of thanks for Dhenu. He stood outside in the main garden and waited. After a while, Banto came out and dismissively handed him some more coins, saying, "Bakshish." Dhenu had earned cash through this adventure but somehow it didn't satisfy him. Had he been too presumptuous in expecting friendship, or at least recognition?

The days that followed saw a reduction in the spats between the couple, but still, there were occasional wars of words. While the memsahib now seemed more poised, the sahib seemed to lose his composure more with every passing day. He grew moody, irritable, and at times, crazed. And then suddenly out of the blue, the British officer died. They say that after his morning tea he went to the bathroom and never came out. He was found lying there, with his face blue and body erect.

"A clear-cut case of dhatura poisoning," Ram the cook declared with one look at the body. Yet he refused to admit that the morning tea could have been poisoned. "I made the tea with my own two hands," he said indignantly.

While the entire Circuit House and the village was in a state of mayhem, Dhenu caught an occasional glimpse of Margaret, whose poise in the midst of tragedy struck him as strange. "These angrez people have strange ways of expressing their emotions," his mother explained to him. "They laugh and sing to deal with grief. They cry when joyful."

A couple of months later Margaret moved to England on the arm of an eligible young army officer. It was after this, during the deep cleaning of the Circuit House before the next family moved in, that an empty taveez was discovered in the bedside table next to Margaret's bed.

"Only Banto could have known the real purpose of the taveez, but she had left the house right after the sahib's death, grief-stricken. The taveez was tossed into the pile of rubbish, and everyone thought the tale had ended there."

So engrossed was Ramesh in the story that he almost missed a creak on the floorboards of the porch. He instinctively looked behind him to see if Dhenu chacha had more audience. But there was no one there. Ramesh felt his hair stand on end.

Dhenu chacha was gazing towards a distant hill, oblivious to Ramesh's thumping heart. "Everyone believed that Margaret had taken the man's life. They even wondered if they were married at all."

"But why didn't she just go back home? It's not that tough for a couple to separate in their society. I've read this in many books," Ramesh said, to reassure Dhenu chacha that he understood how the grown-up world worked.

Dhenu chacha smiled slyly, "But she did not, because Margaret loved sahib."

Dhenu Chacha recounted the conversations he had overheard between the cook and housekeeper regarding another lady who was frequently mentioned during the couple's fights.

"Anyway, two days after the taveez had been thrown away, they found it back in the same drawer. The superstitious cleaners decided to leave it there. Since then, more than a few people have seen and heard movement in the house at night. They say the sahib is still looking for her."

"Margaret?" Ramesh whispered, shaking his head sadly.

"But no dear boy—Banto! Margaret was livid that the sahib was having an affair with Banto. In fact, Banto was carrying his child."

Ramesh looked at Dhenu chacha aghast.

"There was a silver tea cup, only one of its kind that sahib preferred for his tea. Banto used to bring tea for sahib every morning and memsahib knew that Banto had the first cup of morning tea along with her husband in the guest room. Margaret would add the dhatura she had obtained from sadhu baba to the second cup of tea every morning on the sly. That cup was meant for Banto. She failed to see what the mix up of cups was doing to her husband as he descended into insanity. Margaret had been unknowingly poisoning her own husband."

The sun was peaking in the sky, and it was past lunchtime. Ramesh sat mesmerized listening to Dhenu chacha, whom he felt he already knew like family. Ramesh accepted an invitation for a quick cup of tea and snacks at Dhenu chacha's tiny outhouse adjoining the garden. There he met chachi, Dhenu chacha's wife. Together they chattered and munched on yummy mathis with achar. Dhenu chacha prattled on about other inhabitants of the Circuit House, which were not nearly as scandalous as the Smiths. But the seed for a story was already sown in Ramesh's mind.

The thrills and chills of this allegedly 'true story' emerged as Papa pointed out the Circuit House to us from the high road above the village Dadhi, and stayed with us on our drive back home.

An Unlikely Maverick

I had a swashbuckling, charismatic, and romantic great-great-grandfather. It is difficult to imagine that a dynamic entity like Shah Baba could be related to Babaji and his brothers who were sensitive, academic, disciplined, and slow-moving. They were a mellow lot, to say the least. The only explanation I can come up with is that Shah Baba's progeny were so overawed by their father that they could never imagine themselves filling his shoes. Ramesh was enamored by the legendary status of Shah Baba, whose birth name was Kundan Mehta.

Ramesh did not get to meet Shah Baba because Shah Baba died at the ripe age of fifty-five, leaving behind his two doting wives and three sons. But tales of his deeds were oftentimes repeated, and

Ramesh was a most willing audience for his two dadis (grandmas), who loved to recount stories sprinkled with gallantry, belly dancing damsels, mountain robbers, knives and blades... the list was unending.

In those days, before Ramesh was born, traders would travel from the northern parts of India to Kabul, Afghanistan. This journey through towns, forests, and hills was made on horses, with an extra horse per person to carry tradable goods. These goods included hand-woven cotton cloth and dhurries, warm woolen pattus, blankets, jaggery, and the like.

At Kabul, Shah Baba mingled with traders from Russia, China, Kutch, and central Asia. Here, Shah Baba was a small fish amidst the wealthy and snazzy traders who travelled with entourages of servants and animals. What Baba got in return was gold and silver coins and the much-valued dry fruits—cashews, dates, raisins, and almonds. These were hard to come by in Kamahi.

"Almond trees were first planted by your Babaji in Kamahi," Ramesh's dadi had told him. Shah Baba had gifted a few saplings to the carpenter's son, who made a happy profit growing an orchard with these. There was also a collection of exotic knickknacks that each of the dadis had zealously treasured—a Russian hat, a Chinese good-luck charm, a jade bracelet, a dervish's taveez and a turquoise necklace secured from friendly mountain nomads.

His adventurous junkets to Kabul and the fact that he had married twice—something unheard of in the community—explained his title of Shah Baba, which means someone who lives like a king. Ramesh never tired of the stories about Shah Baba. On winter nights, in the flickering light of the oil lamp, wrapped in a pattu, he would go to sleep listening to stories of the adventures of Shah Baba as one of the grandmas rocked him. The clean and dry-caked mud walls of the house provided him comfort that permeated every cell in his body.

Of the two dadis, the older one was Ramesh's 'real' grandma. But an onlooker would perceive it differently. The younger dadi, or Choti, as she was commonly known, would engulf Ramesh in a hug every time she saw him. She stole sweet treats for him, and saved extra slices of mango and spoonfuls of butter, despite a hawk-eyed Mata. Sometimes Ramesh wondered if Choti did this just to spite Mata, but he could not detect a bit of meanness in the fair, shiny, and dimpled face of Choti.

One day when he returned from school, he was ushered into a room where all the younger kids sat glumly. Choti had passed on. Many things were said, muttered, whispered about her, of which Ramesh understood none.

"Serves her right for marrying her sister's husband," Mata had said bitterly to bua, while patting a sobbing Ramesh.

"She was not all there."

"I caught her wandering in her under-things once."

The stories became more vicious and fictitious with every whisper. Even Nikku, Ramesh's best friend, made a snide comment he had picked up from his mother, who was Mata's close friend.

Unable to listen to any more gossip about Choti, Ramesh began to avoid the chatty groups of women and kids. He decided to hang around Babaji and his brothers, or to ruminate alone with the silent, non-judgmental animals around the barn.

A week after Choti's death, as Ramesh sat with Sheru, his grandma sat down heavily next to him and ruffled his hair for the first time in his memory.

"I will miss her as much as you," she said, her eyes welling up. Ramesh leaned into her as she put an arm around his shoulders. "She was the best. And I will tell you a secret that no one else knows."

"That's it! She will tell me I am really adopted like Krishan chacha or an illegitimate grandson of Choti," Ramesh thought as he braced himself for the news. When it comes to secrets, for children, logic is like a kite caught in capricious winds—a harum-scarum of possibilities.

"They are right, Choti was not all there," dadi said as Ramesh looked up at her horrified.

"You too, dadi?" he asked. Dadi shook her head.

"But it doesn't matter, because both Shah Baba and I loved Choti. In fact, she is the reason Shah Baba and I got married. That is the secret that remained between Shah Baba and me."

"Ramesh, finish your schoolwork," Mata came up from behind them, right on cue.

"This is the best story about Shah Baba. I will tell you later. Go do your schoolwork or your mother will descend on me like a banshee," dadi said. Ramesh was amazed by the cruel things mothers-in-law and daughters-in-law could say about each other in one breath, and then be perfectly fine with each other the next.

But the talk with dadi had reassured Ramesh. His grandma held no rancor against her sister for having married Shah Baba. What other people said did not matter.

Many days had passed after this conversation when Ramesh spotted dadi sitting alone shelling fresh green peas into a bowl. In situations like this, Choti would thrust the smallest, softest, and sweetest peas into Ramesh's palm. He sobered and sat next to dadi and started shelling the peas to help her. She patted his head.

"You said there was a story about Shah Baba and Choti?" Ramesh reminded dadi. She stopped for a moment, then nodded and got back to the shelling. The pile of pea pods was huge. These peas would be stored in the cool mud house where all the drinking water pots were kept.

"Choti was different from the beginning. She had the habit of staring at people's faces. The funny part is, no matter how long she stared, she learned nothing of what others expected of her," dadi said with a faraway look in her eyes. She shook her head like someone who has given up trying to solve a puzzle.

"I suspect she stared to understand why she felt so different from everyone around her. She would laugh a little too much when she saw everyone laughing, even if she hadn't understood what they were laughing about. Everything she did to decrease the distance between herself and the normal world, actually increased the chasm even more. Everyone had started calling her 'jhalli,'" dadi said. A shadow passed over her usually jolly face.

"But she was not like that at all!" Ramesh exclaimed. "She had a very sharp memory, and she even helped me with school math!"

"Even the village grocer is good at math, dear boy. But if you don't learn to play the social game, you are a goner, a good for nothing, the butt of all jokes," dadi said with a sigh.

"But I could never tell," Ramesh said, his voice softened by the shock of learning this truth.

"That is because she taught herself to disguise her actual identity, her feelings. It's easier for girls, though not less traumatic," dadi said. "All she had to do was stay quiet."

What dadi was telling Ramesh was remarkably similar to Krishan chacha's situation. Krishan chacha hadn't learned to play the social game either, and had to withstand jeers and mocking. Ramesh thought back to the times when Choti would sit, quiet and disinterested, in a corner during family discussions. Usually, Ramesh would perch on her lap or lay next to her with his head in her lap.

Black clouds had gathered in the sky, and a robust dusty wind suddenly began to blow. Ramesh helped dadi gather the peas, ran to safely store them in the mud house, and then back again to dadi, who was slowly plodding to the kitchen. The kitchen was a separate unit in the house, a hut of sorts, on one side of the courtyard.

Afternoon tea was being served. Dadi picked up her cup and sat on the edge of the covered porch connected to the kitchen. The porch served primarily as the dining room for the household where men, children, and women ate meals in turns. Teatime was the only time of the evening when everyone mingled, regardless of the family segment, gender, or age.

"What happened then?" Ramesh asked as Mata handed him a deep brass tumbler filled with freshly boiled milk.

"My father was a very progressive man for the ages we lived in," dadi said.

"Tai, what stories are you feeding the child?" It was Kumkum, Ramesh's bua, an aunt he despised because of her quick wit and vicious tongue.

"At least someone wants to hear what I have to say," Dadi mumbled, her toothless mouth breaking into a smile that even Kumkum found hard to resist. She backed into the kitchen, leaving Ramesh and dadi alone.

"My father knew that if Choti got married, she would be doomed to neglect and possible exploitation. If she remained unmarried, she would be the odd sister, the spinster of the household, ridiculed by all."

"So he asked Shah Baba to marry both of you?" Ramesh asked, his eyes round with wonder. Dadi shook her head and chortled.

"Your Shah Baba looked like an angrez!" dadi said. She stared into space. Ramesh imagined dadi sketching Shah baba's face against the dark and heavy clouds that threatened to crack open at any moment.

Ramesh had heard that Shah baba was handsome but had only seen handmade portraits of him. He kept quiet. They listened to the soft stirring of the leaves of the large neem tree in the courtyard. Dadi seemed to have travelled back in time.

"My father met Kundan on a trip to Kabul. He was a young hand with one of the traders at that time. Impressed by his stately bearing and flair for negotiating, my father invited Kundan home. He planned to offer my hand in marriage to him," dadi said, and tilted her cup to pour some tea into the saucer. She slurped at it noisily. Her hollow cheeks sucked in further when she upturned the dish to empty it into her mouth.

She looked like a toothless, wrinkled baby. Ramesh waited patiently, watching her with great fondness.

"To reach our village one must cross a deep khad dotted with stones of all sizes, the underground water of the khad producing a musical gurgling sound, sweeter than you could ever hear," dadi said before taking the next big slurp of tea. Ravines filled with stones and pebbles called khads were a regular feature of the region's topography. Every khad was different just like no two snowflakes are the same. Kamahi had its own khad that lay across flat land outside the village. It would fill up during the monsoon but was never half as romantic as the one described by dadi.

"Choti used to love hanging out here with a book or two in her hand. The river, the birds, and nature never judged her."

Dadi stopped talking and wiped away the stream of tears running down one cheek.

"The water was high in the khad that day when Kundan was to visit us." Ramesh did not like where the story was headed and pretended to sip his milk thoughtfully.

"In trying to catch a better look at the future groom of her sister, Choti, who sat on an enormous boulder, leaned too far and fell into the water. She broke her ankle, and thankfully, nothing more," dadi chuckled, though her cheeks were still wet with tears.

"Choti told me later that Kundan risked his life and saved her. He carried her back home. I hid behind the curtain and watched my smitten little sister refusing to let go of Kundan's arms," dadi said.

"Tai is making it all up," Kumkum said as she came up behind them. She pinched Ramesh's red cheeks. "Tai, you are embarrassing the child with your love stories."

"I am telling nothing but the truth. You girls think with your long hair and slim waists you are the only young women the world will ever see? Choti and I were prettier than any of you," dadi shot at Kumkum and two other buas.

The conversation was taking a turn for the worse, threatening to smudge dadi's credibility. Ramesh resented Kumkum bua even more.

"Bua, Anandini is picking sequins off your pink dupatta!" Ramesh said to Kumkum bua to distract her and preserve dadi's nostalgic mood. As expected, Kumkum bua rushed to find Ramesh's little sister, Anandini. Dadi had started to hum a song and seemed to forget the story.

"Dadi?" Ramesh tapped her with his finger. She stopped singing.

"You know that big wooden chest where your mother hoards everything?" she said. Ramesh knew that chest. He and Anandini had nicked many a sweet treat from it, unknown to Mata. And he understood what his dadi meant by hoarding. There were articles in that chest that were many kinds of precious. It was a treasure chest in every possible way, with a chunky iron lock guarding its contents.

"Choti was smuggled into this house in that dowry trunk," dadi whispered into Ramesh's ears. Ramesh stared at her, and then together they burst out laughing.

"Everyone thought that Shah Baba had been greedy and had married two beautiful sisters for the dowry. But that is not true. My father would have never agreed to marry both his daughters to the same man! So that day when Kundan came visiting us, I made him promise that he would marry my sister too so I could take care of her."

"But why did he agree to it?" Ramesh wondered.

"He had fallen in love with me," dadi said, patting Ramesh's cheek. In spite of dadi's toothless mouth and wrinkles, a blush appeared on her face.

"Choti arrived in the trunk, and once here my father had to allow the wedding to save face. They called the priest, and a secret marriage ceremony took place for Choti and Kundan. If it were not for your Shah baba, my sister would have been lost to me forever, and I would have lived a miserable life. It was not his travels and trading acumen that made him a true hero in my eyes."

Dadi had been right. This was the most intriguing story about Shah baba that Ramesh had ever heard. While tales of his adventures were many, this little gem turned out to be his favorite.

The Baoli

Mankind's biggest fear is the unknown. We meet the unknown in many forms—uncertainty of the future, the fill-in-the-blank after death, the secrets that darkness and silence hold, and all the inexplicable acts of mankind. Yet life presses on. Inside us and around us the new replaces the old, and the mystery of the unknown continues.

    Nainu feared the unknown. She had picked this fear from her grandmother who had lived to a hundred, leaving behind a petrified teenaged granddaughter who ate food only after circling her plate with water to ward off the evil eye, sprayed water over her own head to keep negative energies away, and spent half her day praying to the deities. Nainu's biggest fear was what her fate would be after she got married.

Ramesh knew Nainu only as someone who hung out with Kumkum bua and other young women in the family. He shared this story with us because Nainu was married to someone who lived in my mother's maternal village, Ganari.

Since I got to know Nainu's story much later, when she was no more, you could say, her unknown was familiar to me. For the reader's sake I could say that her unknown was warm and kindly. But when have idealistic wishy-washy lives made for good stories?

Nainu had heard horrifying stories about girls who got married into villages far from home—beaten for dowry, and forced to have many, many children. She had recently turned sixteen and her parents had started looking for a match for Nainu, whose beauty was talked about by the officious matchmaking aunties in the community. She had milky white skin, a nose so sharp it could give a needle good competition, and a heart-shaped face with a mole on lower left side of her chin. She had been named Nainu for her soft brown doe eyes with heavy lashes.

She stood taller than most girls in the village but frequently crouched low so she could disappear amongst other girls her age when she noticed someone staring at her. However, it was a hard task to duck down when she was walking with heavy brass pots filled with water balanced on her head. This was when Nainu's perfectly shaped body, her swan-like neck, and thickly braided hair that swung at her hips were hard to miss for any onlooker, man or woman. Nainu hated the attention. Other girls hated the attention Nainu received. Friendless, she had stuck to her dadi's side like a pocket puppy till dadi had passed away the year before.

"Only the luckiest girls get well-meaning and kind husbands. Most men just want someone to abuse to feel good about themselves," dadi had told her. The unknown grew more sinister for Nainu every time dadi warned her of this.

From time to time, however, she noticed a young man whose eyes followed her. In those days one knew everyone in the village, as well as the frequent visitors from nearby areas. But no one knew this boy. One of the girls, less jealous of Nainu than the others, pointed him out to her.

"He is at the well near that tree every Tuesday and Friday," the girl said. Nainu pulled the dupatta billowing from beneath the water pot on her head, and clenched it between her teeth to hide her face from the boy. If she told her father about the young man, he would round up the villagers to beat him up. But that was not the problem for Nainu because she felt no connection with the boy. The incident would call attention to her, and she didn't want her family to turn into grist for the village's rumor mill.

One day, while returning from the family's vegetable patch with a basket containing carrots, radishes, onions and a cauliflower balanced precariously on her head, Nainu stopped short when she saw someone leaning against a tree fifty paces from her house. The boy swooshed the air with a thin stringy stick. The sound must have masked Nainu's footfall, for he seemed unaware of her approach.

Even though the pots of water were heavy, they were easier to carry compared to baskets of vegetables, which tipped at any hint of wind. Her father loved cauliflower paratha, and Nainu planned to make it for him to provide her mother a break from kitchen work.

Nainu clutched the basket and started walking slowly past the tree.

The young man who followed her without ever talking to her stood with his back propped against the tree trunk. Just as a twig broke under Nainu's foot, he looked up, startled, and comically fell onto his side. Nainu couldn't suppress a burst of laughter. The boy formed an L shape with his right hand to collect the mop of his hair which having fallen over his forehead had covered his eyes. He swept his hair back tucking them firmly behind his ears. This would have been Nainu's window for escape. Home was just a sprint away, but she stood mesmerized by the simplicity of the movement of the boy's hand and his comical fall. She did not feel threatened by him.

The boy stood up. He held something in his left fist. He opened the fist and offered the object to Nainu. She recognized it as her silver anklet, which she had lost on one of her trudges to the village well. Her face burning with shyness, she took the anklet, murmured thanks, and ran home without a word.

Nainu started looking forward to Tuesdays and Thursdays, when she would see the boy waiting for the girls to pass. He came religiously and stood still, as if silently offering prayers to the deity he worshipped. Nainu never looked his way. But if he missed a day, she felt perturbed. Her appetite disappeared and voices around her turned into meaningless cacophony. When she saw him silhouetted against the tree again, the normal rhythm of the universe would resume for her. Fear of the unknown still consumed her, but the boy did not belong to that unknown. He felt familiar.

When a marriage proposal came for her from Ganari, a village known far and wide for Mauni baba's shrine, Nainu's heart skipped a beat. Mauni baba had pledged his life to penance and had also taken a vow of silence. Nothing could go wrong in a place blessed by a holy presence. The ominous unknown would have no place there.

A flurry of wedding-related activity followed her shy nod to the proposal. Saris were bought from Talwada, jewelry from Jalandhar. The officious aunties who had missed their bounty came, and took Nainu's face in their hands, shaking their heads. "She could have found a prince," they said.

Nainu had not yet met the man she was to marry, but in her heart she knew that her dead dadi would be convinced that it was the right decision. In fact, whenever she saw the boy waiting on the path to the village well after that, he seemed like a token of her bright future. She even smiled at him once under the guise of giggling with the other girls.

"Nainu will no longer go to the well to fetch water. We don't want a twisted ankle or a broken wrist a week from the wedding," her father said one day. This was when it hit Nainu that she wouldn't get to see the boy again. Her heart agonized strangely, angrily. What was that? She did not know.

During the week of her imprisonment at home, everything grew colorless. Even the thought of Mauni baba did not cure the gloomy sepia shade that bled from her past towards her future. From the upper deck of the cowshed at home, she saw the boy appear at dawn near the same tree where he had given back her anklet. He left when night fell. This continued every day that week. He did not approach her, or her family. On the day of the wedding, the boy was not there. Nainu went through the motions of the onerous traditions of a Hindu wedding like a clockwork doll. "A man from Ganari will be kind and well-meaning," she repeated to herself as her bedecked palanquin reached the village she had married into. Enamored by Ganari, Nainu had agreed to the wedding knowing nothing about her future husband or his family.

She woke up the next morning to find herself amidst tittering strangers. She mentally hugged her dadi, changed into her old silver anklets, and stepped into the new and alien environment.

At the beginning, her husband, who was ten years older than her, seemed kind. Her mother-in-law, always smiling, appeared well-meaning. The family well-off. "This is all Mauni baba's blessing," Nainu told herself as she visited the holy saint's shrine the next day. It was a plain white-domed structure as tall as Nainu herself. Inside, it held a fading sketch of a sadhu made with coal. Nainu memorized the face, took a deep breath, closed her eyes and placed Mauni baba next to her dadi on the altar in her mind.

When one is in love with an idea, anything and anybody can slip into its glow and appear lustrous.

It was when she discovered calluses on her hands, blisters on her feet, and dark circles under her eyes that Nainu took another look at the life she was living. Her day started at four-thirty in the morning. She cleaned the cowshed, fetched water from a faraway baoli, swept the kitchen, prepared breakfast, swept the dyodhi and the courtyard, prepared lunch, fed the cows, plucked vegetables from the kitchen garden, laid out beds for the family, and prepared dinner. She watched her dadi weep in her mind, speechless and disillusioned. Dadi had not known that despite caution, the unknown could still be cruel.

Nainu wiped her dadi's tears and focused on Mauni baba, for he had provided her the fortitude to endure all of this for two years. But the worst was yet to come. Nainu had been unable to bear a grandchild.

The best part of Nainu's day was fetching water from the grand baoli of Ganari. While no one could remember the exact year the step-well had been dug, they said it had been there even when "kings ruled the land." That was enough for Nainu, for she had no education of history, freedom, or women's rights. Though the construction was chunky in style, there were flower patterns and human shapes carved on the stone-paneled corners of the baoli. She believed these were the kings and queens of the past.

Fifty steps down led you to the underground water, which tasted sweet and cool. For Nainu, every morning felt like she had dipped the smoldering iron of her emotions into the baoli's cool waters, which endowed her spirit with strength. At times, she sat on the steps contemplating the fickle nature of the unknown—the way she had tried to run away from it and how it had caught up with her, with its demon's fangs, horns, and forked tail.

Another daughter-in-law from the village also woke up very early to fetch water from the baoli. Glad to have found each other, the two girls forged a friendship out of their shared pain, though they never talked about it. Rather, this girl whose house Nainu would never visit, filled in Nainu on Ganari's gossip.

"Did you know that no theft has ever taken place in Ganari," she told Nainu one day. "They say that Mauni baba's spirit settles like a boulder on anyone who tries to steal anything from anyone."

Nainu would often visit Mauni baba's shrine to silently ask him questions. But she blamed no one, neither her dadi nor Mauni baba. Her marriage had been her choice.

One morning, Nainu left early to fetch water from the baoli. The previous evening, her mother-in-law had been particularly nasty to Nainu's father, who had brought gifts for Nainu and her new family. Her distraught father had not met her eyes when he left. He had refused to stay the night, and left his cup of tea half-finished.

She carefully put down the two earthen pots on the twenty-fifth step on the way down to the water, and lay her head on arms folded around her knees. Then she wept. She did not know why the tears flowed, for girls in those days were brought up to have no expectations from life other than to have children. Her mother-in-law did not let a day go by without making a snide remark about Nainu not having conceived. "If my boy had married that girl from Talwada, I'm sure I would have a grandson playing in my lap by now."

But Nainu did not want to have any children. Shame, anger, and helplessness make a deadly cocktail for someone who has a watery escape before their eyes each day. "No one knows the depth of this baoli. It has existed for hundreds of years. Imagine the tales it could tell," her chatty daughter-in-law friend had reflected one day.

The early morning breeze caressed her hair, but Nainu's shoulders shook with sobs as her dadi's reassuring image blurred in her mind. Spent from crying, she took a deep breath and looked at the placid, inviting waters of the baoli, darkened at places by shadows cast by the steps and pillars. Shadows, sharp in daylight, don't disappear at night. Rather they turn into guardians of sinister secrets.

With her entire day packed with chores, this was the only time she could spare to collect water from the baoli. The water near the far corner reflected a movement in the shadow cast by the pillar on the opposite side. She looked up as a figure started walking on the stairs adjacent to where she sat. It was still dark and the stars still held their fort in the early morning sky. Nainu detected a figure with a long beard and shoulder length hair like Mauni baba. Was this a hallucination or a visitation from a spirit? Perhaps she had gone mad.

In a few seconds she could see who was there. His body was a picture of neglect, but his eyes were alive with the same passion and directness they radiated when they had followed her in the village back home.

"Why didn't you stop my marriage?" she asked.

He shrugged.

"Are you deaf?" Nainu screamed, surprised at herself.

"I thought I did not deserve you."

"Then why are you here now?" Nainu asked, and picked up the brass pots and started climbing down the low steps. The other miserable daughter-in-law could arrive at any time, and Nainu's life had no place for scandal.

The boy followed her down, helped her fill the earthen pots, and placed one on her head. He carried the other pot on his own head, holding Nainu's hand as they ascended the stairs. Nainu had never felt so happy and conflicted at the same time. Once they reached the edge of the baoli, he placed the second pot in the nook of her arm, over her waist.

"I will wait here at midnight for you today," he said, and hurried away.

Nainu watched him shuffle away. Three years of marriage had taught her to discern between sincere and ersatz body language. This boy had not changed. But Nainu had lost faith in herself. She had come to detest the unknown because of her fear of it. The unknown could disguise itself. It had woven a web to trap her, to teach her that it could not be escaped.

But this boy was part of another world, a different unknown. Could it be possible to love the unknown?

She shook off the feeling. The man had invited her to elope with him that night. Nainu knew what her dadi would say, so she refused to consult her. She firmly placed aside any thoughts about the unknown.

It was still early morning. She visited Mauni baba's shrine. She sat staring at his picture in a crumbling wooden frame, surrounded with flowers and offerings from the day before. Finally, she cleaned the space, touched her head to the floor, and headed home with her water pots. During the day, she sat through the taunts flung at her by her mother-in-law, sister-in-law, and aunts about her father and family, as if in a trance.

She finished sweeping the kitchen around 11:30 pm that night. She was sweaty, disheveled, and tired, but a strange vitality coursed through her. She looked at the full moon, removed her silver anklets, clenched them tightly in her hands, and crept through the courtyard where the men slept on manjis. Her heart jumped into her throat when someone caught her hand. It was her father-in-law. His eyes were first confused, then enraged. He must have read her body language. He was about to say something that would have woken up the household when something remarkable happened. The unknown showed up.

Her robust father-in-law could not speak. He tried to rise from the bed but fell back on his manji as if a heavy weight had landed on his chest. He let go of Nainu's hand and started clutching his throat. Anyone who saw the scene would think someone was sitting on the man and strangling him.

Mauni baba's spirit settles like a boulder on anyone who tries to steal anything from anyone…

Nainu shimmied through the scattered beds occupied by snoring family members, her body shivering with fear, and ran towards the baoli, slipping into a fall a few times in the darkness. What if the man whose name Nainu did not know was not there? Then the baoli would be her new home. Her toe struck a stone, but she hurried on without a wince.

She reached the baoli, whose still waters reflected the moon. The man stood there waiting with a horse's reins in his hands. He interlaced his fingers, fashioning a step for Nainu to haul herself up onto the horse. The two fled into the darkness. In hindsight, she had known deep down that they would end up together.

But why had Mauni baba helped her escape? If he prevented thefts in the village, he should have aided her draconian father-in-law in stopping her, for this man had purloined her. The mystery blended itself into the unknown, which did not scare Nainu anymore. She had fallen in love with it.

Afterword

These stories transport me to the foggy winter nights, lush summer hillsides, and carefree days of childhood spent in my father's village every time I read them. Writing down these memories has been more of a cathartic experience than a literary one.

Papa left Kamahi Devi when he went to Agra for college and then to Panjab University to study Law. He lived in big cities later on, but Kamahi was woven into the fabric of his life. I have worked hard to present these stories in an authentic manner though I am aware that this may not be entirely possible. After all, these are stories of my father's childhood as seen through my eyes.

Still, everyone can relate to these tales as they capture day-to-day situations. While they may be region-specific, the feelings portrayed are universal. They also provide a refreshing look at life in the hills of Himachal, in the post-independence days.

Glossary

With Love from Pitpita

Pitpita - a made-up term of endearment used by the protagonist for the author

Swimming with the Buffaloes

Toba - village pond

mata - Hindi term for 'mother'

chappals - slippers

babaji - Hindi term for grandfather

budh - a makeshift wooden gate that leads into fields

dupatta - a long and wide scarf worn by women in India

mochi - shoemaker / cobbler

pedas - a sweet treat prepared in thick, semi-soft pieces using condensed milk, sugar and traditional flavorings like cardamom seeds, nuts, and saffron

Nandi and a Tonga Ride

tonga - a light, two-wheeled, horse-drawn vehicle used in India, rarely seen nowadays

bua - paternal aunt/father's sister

chacha - paternal uncle generally father's younger brother; also used as an informal way of addressing any man who is around one's father's age

pakhi - hand-held fan

sharara - a pair of loose pleated trousers worn by women, typically with a long shirt and dupatta

aam ki chutney - mango chutney

phuphaji - paternal aunt's husband / bua's husband

manji - old Indian style bed made of woven net or rope mesh; also called Charpai

Mangtu Baba's House

baba - a familiar form of address for elderly men

batti - cotton wicks used in oil lamps

ghoonghat - a Hindi term for a type of veil or headscarf worn by Indian women to cover their heads

paratha - stuffed Indian flatbread

hukkah - a tobacco pipe with a long, flexible tube used to draw smoke through a jar of water which cools it

Ram-ram baba - a form of 'hello' for elderly men

roti - Indian flatbread prepared and eaten fresh

Papa and Sheru

chota - in Hindi means 'small'

mathi - salty, deep-fried flour snacks

pattu - hand-woven woolen blankets that are turned into coats, dresses or ponchos

chacha - father's younger brother's wife

dyodhi - the room situated at the entrance of a house meant to keep the personal quarters separate from the outer facing part of the house

baoli - a step-well / an underground water reservoir reached by descending a steps

gaggar - brass pots used to store water

Bheenda's Little Secret

mochi - shoemaker / cobbler

brahmin - a member of the Hindu caste of brahmins

Krishan Chacha

Kamahi Devi - Located around 40 km from Hoshiarpur, this temple town is dedicated to goddess Kamakshi. It is located in the village of Beh Nangal and is said to have been built by the Pandavas

baoli - a step-well

chulha - a small earthen or brick stove built on the ground

masterni - female teacher

mama - a form of address for maternal uncle, i.e., mother's brother

murga - a form of physical punishment meted out to children in schools in those days. The position resembles a rooster as it involves squatting and then looping the arms behind the knees and firmly holding the ears

For the Love of Mata!

mata - a familiar form of address for 'mother'

pinni - a type of sweet dessert made from ghee, wheat flour, jaggery and almonds

amla murabba - Indian goose berries cooked in sugar syrup, flavored with cardamom, saffron, black pepper and black salt

khatai - an eggless cookie prepared with ghee, refined flour, semolina, gram flour, and sugar

Circuit House

Cheer Dee Khui - a bus stop on Talwada road in Punjab

mandir - a temple

Madhubala - a Bollywood actress of 1950-60s

dhajji walls - thought to be derived from a Persian word meaning "patchwork quilt wall" and is a traditional building type found in the western Himalayan region

phirangi - a foreigner, in those days a term used for Britishers

mithai - confectionery and desserts

halwai - confectioner who crafts mithai

jalebi - a popular mithai made by deep frying flour batter and soaking it in sugar syrup

nautanki - folk operatic theatre performance

gulli-danda - a traditionally popular outdoor game among children; Indian variation of 'Tip-cat'

Pahari - colloquial term for people hailing from Himachal Pradesh gora - Hindi for fair-skinned, typically Britishers in those times

sahib - Hindi for 'Sir'

memsahib - Hindi for 'Madam'

Baisakhi - denoting the month of the Hindu lunar year, regarded as the start of the new year

sadhu - a holy man, sage, or ascetic

tantrik - a follower of tantra or the esoteric traditions of Hinduism, associated with black magic

paise - monetary unit in India

angrez - a Britisher

taveez - amulet

bakshish - a tip, gratuity

dhatura - a poisonous plant belonging to the night-shade family also known as Datura.

An Unlikely Maverick

Shah - a king or kingly

pattu - blankets/throws made of wool

dadi - grandma

jhalli - a negative term used to mean 'feeble-brained'

khad - stony ravine that fills up with water during rains

dupatta - a long and wide scarf worn by women in India

tai - a form of address for father's older brother's wife, also a familiar term for older women in the family

The Baoli

Talwada, Jalandhar - cities in North India

manji - rope-mesh bed

You Write. We Publish.

To publish your own book, contact us.

We publish poetry collections, short story collections, novellas and novels.

contact@thewriteorder.com

Instagram- thewriteorder

www.facebook.com/thewriteorder

www.ingramcontent.com/pod-product-compliance
Lightning Source LLC
LaVergne TN
LVHW010344070526
838199LV00065B/5790